BROKEN WARRIORS

LOVE BUILDS A BRIDGE

A CJT CHRISTIAN ROMANCE

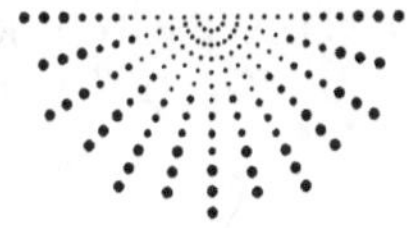

CYNTHIA JO TERRELL

ZAMIZ PRESS

FICTION / Christian / General

FICTION / Christian / Romance / Suspense

Special discounts are available on quantity purchases by corporations, associations and others. For details, contact the author.

This book is a work of fiction. Any references to events, people, or places are used fictitiously. Names, characters, places and events are products of the author's imagination, and any resemblances to actual events or places or persons, living or dead, is entirely coincidental.

DO YOU HAVE A MESSAGE TO SHARE WITH THE WORLD?
ARE YOU INTERESTED IN HAVING YOUR BOOK PUBLISHED?
VISIT ZAMIZPRESS.COM

To Liz,
my inspiration for this book

"Love Lifted Me"

CHAPTER ONE

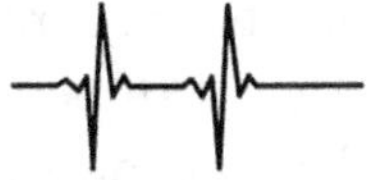

Warm spring air whipped Jessie's dark hair into wavy tangles as she turned onto the highway leading to Claymon. In less than two weeks she would marry the love of her life. Jordan had worked his way into her heart, guiding her back to the faith she'd run from. With a smile, she cranked up the music and sang along.

A loud rumble jolted her car, and she clenched her fingers around the steering wheel. Her Mustang's undercarriage ground into the pavement. She squeezed her eyes shut as her front wheel rolled down the highway in the path of oncoming traffic. Screeching tires pierced her ears and forced her eyes open as a pickup careened into her lane. She braked hard, twisted the wheel and skidded toward the trunk of a massive tree. "Here's where I get hurt," flashed through her mind.

Darkness threatened as she struggled to make sense of the sounds swirling above her.

"Call 911!"

"She nearly hit my car!"

"Her wheel came right at me. Unbelievable!"

Jessie moaned as blackness enveloped her.

* * *

Jordan Raycom sat at his desk finishing paperwork when the alarm blasted. A vehicle had plowed into a tree on the main road into town. Dropping his work, he sprinted to join his team of three. He hopped in beside the driver and rechecked the location as Phil tore out of the garage.

"Jessie might be caught in this mess. She's headed to the florist this morning."

Phil met his eyes. "She might. I bet this causes a huge traffic jam."

The paramedics came upon the scene where a squad car sat with lights flashing. Jordan's heart leaped to his throat at the sight of the crumpled vehicle. No, it can't be. He sprang from the ambulance and stumbled to the ground. Scrambling to his feet, he shouted in a voice he barely recognized as his, "It's Jessie!" Sprinting to the Mustang, he tugged with fury on the unyielding door. "Jessie! Hang on, Love. We'll get you out!" He spun around. "Somebody bring the glass breaker. Now!"

A strong arm grabbed his shoulders. "Jordan!" Phil commanded and waited until Jordan met his eyes. "Step back, man. Get yourself under control." Jordan twisted his arm, but Phil tightened his grip. "Remember what you always tell us."

Jordan understood the look in his partner's eyes and backed away. He fell to his knees gripping his whirling head. As the lead paramedic, Jordan knew Phil was right. Emotional responses led to deadly mistakes. He closed his eyes for a minute, breathed a prayer and ran to lend assistance.

* * *

A floating sensation engulfed Jessie as hands lifted her onto a hard surface. A voice she should know, but couldn't place, filtered into her confusion. "You're going to be ok. Stay with me, Jessie. Come on, fight for it."

"Jordan?" Jessie gasped as a sharp pain stabbed her above the waist. She tried to shift into a more comfortable position. "My legs." Darkness enveloped her again.

The fog around her brain lifted a bit, and Jessie strained to understand. She heard voices, but not the familiar one she had heard earlier.

"Jordan's driving?" a female's voice murmured.

"Yes, he agreed it was for the best. He's too close to the situation. He needs to concentrate on getting to the hospital and let us attend to the victim."

"Oh," Jessie groaned. She squeezed her eyes and formed raspy words. "Wreck? Jordan?"

"Yes, Jessie, you've been in a wreck," came a soothing voice. "Jordan is up front driving. I'm Phil. Rachelle and I are taking care of you. We're on the way to the hospital. Try to stay awake if you can."

Jessie's mouth moved but only produced a guttural moan. Pain accosted her from every angle, and it took all her energy to remain conscious.

After an eternity, the ambulance doors opened, and the paramedics rolled her through open doors. "Female patient, age 26, with a back injury and possible punctured lung." Darkness overcame her.

* * *

Rays of sunlight peeked around the edges of the window blinds and played on the face of the woman that held Jeremy Marcus' heart. He brushed his lips across the cheek of his new bride. Vikki stirred in her sleep and snuggled her head against his shoulder. Holding her close, he let his mind drift along the road that had brought him to a place where his heart could know love again.

Shannon's death at the hands of drugged-out thugs had catapulted him on an unwanted journey. His young daughter Heather, whom paramedics delivered as his wife lay dying, was the fragile rope he'd clung to for three years as he limped through life, denying the anger and guilt that threatened to emerge from his lifeless soul. That is until Vikki entered his life and played havoc with his heart.[1]

Vikki's eyes fluttered open. He kissed her lips and ran his fingers through her light brown hair. "Hey, baby. Good morning."

"Hi." Vikki smiled, stretched her arms, and snuggled closer, her green eyes melting into his. "You know what? I'm your wife now."

He touched her cheek. "Well, you'd better be, or I'll lose my preaching gig for sure," he grinned and met her lips again.

Later that morning, Jeremy and Vikki sat at a table enjoying brunch in the spacious lobby of the rustic lodge nestled at the foot of the Smoky Mountains. Vikki twisted the cap off a pill bottle and popped a capsule in her mouth, swallowing it with a sip of juice. "My last one," she said. "I still can't believe I got an ear infection at my age."

Jeremy smiled at her. "Well, I guess it happens. Does it bother you anymore?"

"No, not at all." Her eyes grew wide, and she brought a hand to her mouth.

"What's wrong?"

"Nothing. I—I guess I choked for a second. I'm fine now." She returned his smile. "What do you want to do today?"

Jeremy reached for her hands. "Whatever you want. I did have a thought, though."

"What is it?"

"Well, my family came here on vacation several years ago, and we climbed a trail to the Chimney Tops. Jessie and I were young teens, and we loved it." He paused, "It's a bit of a climb, though. It takes an hour or so."

"Sounds great. Let me change into hiking shoes."

Jeremy's phone jingled, and Jordan's name lit up the screen. Jeremy lifted his eyebrows. Why would Jordan be calling? His wisecracking friend probably had some cheeky remark about him being a newlywed. He tapped his phone. "Hey, Jordan, what's up?" Jeremy paled as he listened. "Oh no. Is she ok?"

"What is it?" Vikki whispered and twisted the cross dangling from her necklace.

Jeremy lifted his hand, and his face grew solemn. "A possible severed spine and a punctured lung?" Jeremy stared at Vikki, whose face conveyed her shock. He swept his hand across his blond bangs. "She lost a wheel?" He listened for a few more seconds. "Where is she? Ok, I'll talk to Vikki and call you back."

"What is it?" Vikki repeated louder this time.

"It's Jessie," Jeremy said. "She's been in a wreck. Her wheel fell off the car, and she ran into a tree."

Confusion played on Vikki's features. "Her wheel came off? How could that happen?"

Jeremy shrugged. "I have no idea. The lug bolts must have broken off somehow. Jordan said our mom dropped her off to pick up her car from the auto repair shop this morning and— "

"You said a severed spine. That means…," Vikki inhaled. "We need to go home, right?"

Jeremy's eyes held Vikki's. "I'm sorry. I know it's our honeymoon, but…"

"Of course, we're going home. Jessie's your sister and my friend."

They packed in a rush and loaded the car. "Jeremy, let's pray," Vikki said as she reached for Jeremy's hand. Vikki prayed for Jessie and then pulled her husband into a hug. "It will be ok, Jeremy. I just know it. It has to be." Her voice trembled. "Oh, what if Jessie's paralyzed?"

"Don't go there yet, Vikki. We need to get home and see what's going on." He drew her close. "I love you."

* * *

Jordan, along with Jessie's parents, huddled on a blue upholstered couch in the surgery waiting area of the hospital. Another family sat across the room, living out their particular drama. Jessie's mother spoke to her husband. "Frank, what do you think is taking so long? It's been hours."

He shrugged. "I don't know. Marianne, why don't we get a bite to eat? You're pale and your hands are shaky. Jordan will text us if the doctor comes to talk."

Jordan nodded. "Yeah, go on, you two. I'll stay right here. It could still be awhile."

Marianne hesitated. "Well, ok. We won't be gone

long." She ran her hand across Jordan's shoulders. "Thanks. You can take a break when we get back."

Jordan stood and stretched, walked a few paces, then sat again. A doctor came to talk with the family across the room. Jordan watched as their worried expressions changed to joy, and his mouth formed a slight smile at their good news.

He buried his face in his hands. What was going on with his poor Jessie? Jordan imagined her amber eyes dark with fear. It didn't matter what her injuries were. He would help her through it. "Oh God, please help Jessie. You brought her into my life. Please don't take her away from me."

A quiet peace filled Jordan as he breathed in the presence of God and sensed his voice, "Why do you agonize so, my son? I'm holding Jessie now." He leaned back and closed his eyes.

"Hey, Jordan, we're here."

Jordan jumped in his seat. "Oh, I must have drifted off." He stood and greeted Jeremy and Vikki with a hug. "I'm so glad you guys came." Jordan met Jeremy's eyes and managed a wink and a subtle grin. "Even though it messed with your honeymoon plans."

A faint smile crossed Jeremy's face before he spoke. "So, have you heard anything? Were you there, Jordan?"

"No, not yet, and yes, I was there." His eyes clouded. Jeremy would understand since he worked part-time as a firefighter and EMT. "It's bad, Jeremy. You know what these types of injuries can mean."

"Is she in surgery now?"

Jordan drew in his breath. "Yes, they reinflated her lung, and now they are working on her back."

"Do you think she's paralyzed, Jordan?" Vikki said. "I mean, she's going to make it, right?"

Jordan and Jeremy exchanged glances. "It depends on how severe the injury is. All we can do is wait for now."

"And pray," Jeremy added.

* * *

"No!" Jessie bolted upright and stared at the shadows lurking in the dim light. She squeezed her eyes shut and tried to make sense of her scattered thoughts. Where was she? "Help! Somebody help me!" she screamed into the darkness. A shrill beeping sound was the only response. She yelled out again.

Light flooded the room. "No, don't pull that!" Someone grabbed her hand and held it. "We don't want to have to start another IV."

"Where am I?" Jessie cried and jerked her hand away. "Who are you?"

A soothing voice answered. "You're in the hospital, Jessie. Remember, you were in an accident." The blurry face of a woman looked down at her. "It's alright. I'm your nurse. You're safe here."

Jessie's mind processed this information in bits and pieces. "An accident," she groaned. She rubbed her temples. "My car hit something. Where am I?"

The nurse's voice was gentle. "Yes, you were in a wreck. You're safe in the hospital now. Pain medicines can cause you to be confused. That along with the trauma you've gone through, it's not surprising. I'll talk to your doctor." She straightened Jessie's sheets and tucked the blanket around her shoulders.

"I'm in a black hole. Are people coming to get me?"

"You're not in the hole anymore, Jessie. You're in your room at the hospital."

"Someone took me away for experiments."

"You went for a chest X Ray a while ago, but you're back in your room now."

The nurse pointed to a figurine on the bedside table. "There's your guardian angel. Your mother brought it in for you."

Jessie nodded. "Yes, I see it."

"Whenever you forget where you are, look for your angel, and you'll know you're safe. Try to get some rest. I'll check on you in a bit."

After the nurse left, Jessie picked up the angel and held it close to her heart. Maybe she should sleep with it on her chest. No, the nurse said it would be on the table. She placed it back where it belonged but kept a finger on it until she fell asleep.

-----

1. Read all of Vikki and Jeremy's love story in book one, *Broken Chains*.

CHAPTER TWO

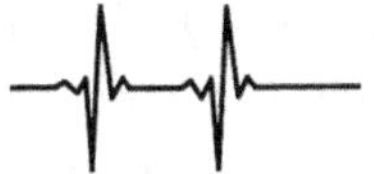

Jordan sat by Jessie's bed in her new room after her stay in the ICU. He knew her mind had cleared enough in the past few hours to comprehend the events that landed her in the hospital.

"But why would my wheel come off?"

Marianne stood at her daughter's bedside and worked at smoothing her sheets. "You don't need to worry about that now, Jessie. Just concentrate on getting well."

Jordan angled his head and peered at Marianne.

"No. I want to know how this all happened," Jessie said. "I was just driving along and —"

"Jessie," Jordan interrupted and walked to the other side of the bed, "Somehow, your lug nuts loosened or snapped. Your wheel fell off and caused your car to skid into a tree." Marianne shot him a look. He paused, took a deep breath, and continued, "But your mother's right. You need to work on getting well."

"My legs are numb. When I touch them, I can't feel

anything." Jessie's eyes darkened, and she looked directly at Jordan. "Do I have a spine injury?"

Marianne spoke before Jordan could answer. "Let's wait for the doctor to talk to you about your condition." She stared at Jordan as if pleading for his silence and patted Jessie's hand. "You need to rest now, dear." Jessie's eyes closed, and she fell silent.

Jordan sighed and met Marianne's eyes. He shook his head, bent close to Jessie's face, and kissed her cheek. "Hang in there, Love. I'll help you figure it all out."

Turning to Marianne, he said, "I'll leave now and let Frank come sit with you."

She nodded her agreement and whispered. "Thanks, Jordan."

Jordan lifted his palms and walked out of the room. He found Frank in the waiting room. "Hey, Frank. Jessie's awake and talking a little bit, but she was drifting off again when I left. I think Marianne could use your company."

"That's good to hear. Jeremy and Vikki will be here right after church." Frank stood and touched Jordan's wrist. "Thanks a lot for everything. You guys saved her."

Jordan shifted his feet. "I'm afraid we weren't able to do enough."

"Jordan, you saved her life. Her injuries were the result of the wreck, nothing else. Jeremy's always telling us how skilled you are."

"Thanks," Jordan patted Frank on the shoulder. "Well, I'm going to get a few hours in at work. I'll be back later this evening." As he walked away, Marianne's voice called out from behind him.

"Wait, Jordan. The doctor came to talk to Jessie. She wants you to be there."

Jordan exchanged a solemn look with Jessie's mother. "Sure, let's go."

Frank joined them, and they made their way to Jessie's room. A man with salt and pepper hair and warm eyes greeted them. "Hello, I'm Dr. Rosen. And you must be Jessie's father and her fiance, Jordan." He shook their hands and motioned toward Jessie. "We are just getting ready to discuss her medical diagnosis."

Jessie gave Jordan a weak smile. The worry etched on her face broke his heart. "Hey, Love, I'm here," he whispered.

Dr. Rosen stood close to Jessie's bed, and Jordan shifted to the other side. The doctor's voice was gentle but confident. "Jessie, you've sustained a severe injury to your spinal cord. That's why you can't feel your legs." He waited for a beat, then continued. "We group vertebrae in sections. In your case, the injury occurred in the upper thoracic vertebrae, which isn't the worst scenario. It is a complete injury, however." He looked into Jessie's round eyes and patted her shoulder.

"What does that mean?" Jessie whispered.

Jordan grew rigid. After years as a paramedic, he didn't have to guess the doctor's answer.

Dr. Rosen's eyes connected with Jordan's for a second before he continued. "It means you have paraplegia. You will most likely have normal arm and hand function, but you are paralyzed from the waist down." He touched Jessie's hand. Marianne's gasp filled the room.

Jessie's face crumpled, and a tear slid down her cheek. "I'll be in a wheelchair forever?"

Dr. Rosen released a puff of air and pulled a chair beside the bed. "Yes, Jessie. There is a chance you can learn to stand in a frame, but your spine is severed.

There are no neuropathways to provide communication between your brain and the injured area. There is some promising new research into therapies that may allow people with complete injuries to stand or even take a few steps with assistance some day. But it remains to be seen if those will be a viable option for you."

He tapped the notes on his clipboard. "I'm sorry, Jessie. We'll do everything we can to help you, and you will be moving to a rehabilitation hospital where professionals will support you as you acclimate to your new situation."

Frank inched closer. "When will that move be made?"

"Early next week, I think." Dr. Rosen touched his patient's hand. "Jessie, I know this is overwhelming news, but you will come to accept your situation and even thrive if you are as strong as I think you are." He stood, glanced at those gathered in the room, then looked back at Jessie. "I'll get the ball rolling on moving you and check in tomorrow."

Jordan sat on the side of the bed and held Jessie as close as possible, taking care not to disturb any tubes. He fought against the tears pooling in his eyes as shock and disbelief played on her face. "It's alright, Jessie. We'll get through this."

He gazed at Jessie's parents, silently huddled as if trying to comprehend the doctor's words. How would they deal with this bombshell?

"Oh, Jordan. I don't know what to do with this," Jessie sobbed against his shoulder.

Jordan stroked her hair. He closed his eyes and wondered how random events could change lives instantly. He'd witnessed more than enough tragedies in his line of work, but they had always fallen on other people. Now tragedy had visited the girl that meant the world to him. He twisted one of her tangled curls as her tears wet his shirt.

* * *

Jessie woke from a fitful sleep to the voice of a nurse beside her. She smiled at Jessie. "I need to get your vitals. How are you feeling this morning?"

Jessie turned her head. The angel stood watch from the bedside table. "I feel a little confused. I had weird dreams last night."

"That's pretty common after several days in the hospital." The nurse glanced at her notes." I believe you will be moving to the rehabilitation hospital soon. That's a good sign."

"What will they do for me there?"

"They will put you to work. You will learn how to take care of yourself in your new circumstances and regain your strength."

Jessie frowned. The nurse touched her arm. "I won't lie to you. It will be hard, and you probably won't care too much for the therapists at first."

"What kind of therapists?"

"You'll have occupational, physical, and probably speech therapy. The nurse touched Jessie's arm. "But you will get through it, and those therapists will become your friends."

Jessie scowled as the nurse turned to leave. "Sounds wonderful," she muttered under her breath.

A few hours later, Jessie was picking at her lunch when Vikki and Jeremy appeared at her door holding a planter of mixed flowers with a teddy bear stuck among the greenery.

"Hi, guys." She gazed at the flower arrangement. The bear held a little sign with the words, "Get well beary soon," written on it. "Thanks. That's cute."

Jeremy tilted his head. "Well, it's not from us. We found it out in the hallway right by your door."

Jessie's lips puckered. "Does it say who sent it?"

Vikki scanned the card. "Hmmm, that's weird. It just says, 'I'm so sorry,' but it doesn't say who it's from." She held the vase out to Jessie.

"I guess whoever it's from must have forgotten to sign it." Jessie turned the card over in her hand. "It's sweet, though. I bet it was Jordan. He knows I like teddy bears." She handed it back to Vikki. "I'll ask him when he comes by."

"I didn't know you liked teddy bears. That doesn't sound like you somehow." Vikki said as she set the flowers on the windowsill.

Jessie leaned forward a bit and shook her head. She tried to look perturbed, but it was too much effort. "It's not something I advertise."

"Oh, don't pretend to be too sophisticated for sweet things like teddy bears. You can't fool me. You're a girly girl underneath it all," Jeremy teased.

Jessie frowned at her brother. "So, teddy bears are my secret pleasure. Just keep a lid on it," she mumbled.

Jeremy grinned at Vikki. "Now, you know the secret, too."

"Oh, stop pestering her, Jeremy. I think it is sweet." She looked back at Jessie. So how are you doing today?"

Jessie closed her eyes and fell back on her pillow. "I don't know. I feel tired and weak."

Vikki reached for her hand. "Of course you do. You've been through a lot."

Vikki and Jeremy visited with Jessie for a few more

minutes while she tried not to close her eyes. Then Vikki stood and gestured to Jeremy. "I think we should let Jessie get some rest, don't you?"

"Yes," he agreed. "Jessie, we'll see you later, ok? Hopefully, you will find out who sent you the planter." Jessie gave him a faint smile.

"I'm sure it was Jordan. He loves to tease."

"You're probably right." Jeremy said as he and Vikki left the room.

CHAPTER THREE

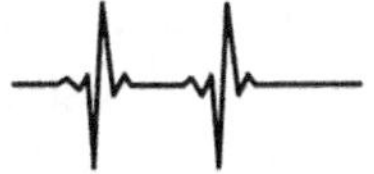

A mber stood in the shop doorway and looked up into the intense brown eyes that held questions she couldn't answer. "I'll be sure to check it out," she promised.

She watched as Jordan strode to his truck after his visit to the shop. The invoice indicated that one of her mechanics installed four tires on a red Mustang, but she couldn't answer why one had fallen off the car. She knew a lug could break off if a mechanic did not set the proper torque on an air wrench or somehow forgot to tighten them. Randy was the service manager, but any of the five mechanics could have installed the tires.

Amber walked out to the service area and studied the men who worked for her. They were all skilled at their job, but mistakes were always possible. Aiden was her newest employee. Had he not tightened the lug nuts properly? She knew that could happen when a mechanic felt rushed or got careless. She sighed. The shop's owner might fire them all over a mistake like this. She spotted Randy, her service manager, and motioned him over.

"Need something?" the weathered mechanic asked as he approached his boss.

"Yes, I need to know who replaced the tires on this vehicle." Amber thrust the invoice toward him.

He glanced at the date. "I can find out. Did the customer have a complaint?"

Amber explained about the accident and her visitor that came looking for answers. "I'm worried, Randy, we can't afford to be sued over a mistake like this. Our new owner might shut the place down. He has other businesses that are probably more profitable than this one. We aren't the only mechanic shop in Claymon anymore."

The wrinkles on Randy's face deepened. "I'll question the guys. Lug nuts can break for other reasons than human error, you know. Think this guy is out for blood?"

Amber sighed. "I don't know. He was polite enough, but direct. He wants answers." Her face clouded. "It was his fiancée who was driving the car, and she's paralyzed now."

"Dang, that's bad. I'll check it out for you."

* * *

Jordan peeked around Jessie's door at Hope Rehabilitation Center to find her sitting grimly on the edge of the bed with the therapist steadying her legs. "How's my beautiful lady? Looks like you're having fun," he said with a tease in his smile.

Jessie's frown told him she wasn't amused. "Becky here decided she needed to torture me this morning."

"I'm pretty sure that's in her job description," he said and winked at the therapist.

Becky laughed. "It will get better. Learning how to balance using the muscles above your waist is important. This is better than the first time, right?"

"I guess. It's all so difficult, though."

"Yes, but you're a fighter. You've only been here a week, and you're already ahead of schedule with your physical therapy goals. You'll be out of here in no time."

Jessie shook her head. "I don't know how. Every day I find some new obstacles to deal with."

"I'm sure it seems that way. This is foreign territory for you. But I promise it will get better if you keep working with the therapists and doctors. Here, let's transfer you to your wheelchair," she continued as she shoved the transfer board under Jessie's hips and helped her move into the chair. "You have determination and grit. That will go a long way in your ability to live a productive and happy life."

Jessie tossed Becky a half-hearted smile and adjusted herself in the wheelchair. "Yeah, I guess. I don't have many options, though, do I?"

"More than you believe right now. And you're making an effort. That's what's important now." Becky backed out of the room. "I'll see you tomorrow morning."

"I'll be here," Jessie said, waving her out the door.

"See you, Becky," Jordan said.

Jordan rested his eyes on Jessie's face. He could read the vulnerability around the edge of her spunkiness. As a paramedic, he had insight into her condition that the average person wouldn't have, and his heart ached for her. Countless hours of therapy and relearning to perform even her most basic needs would make up most of her days in the following weeks. It would take every ounce of courage she could muster to adjust to this new life, and he would be there with her all the way.

Jordan stooped down and gave Jessie an awkward peck on the lips. He stepped back and grinned. "Hey, we've gotta do better than that. I always bend a bit to kiss you, but this is ridiculous." He pulled a chair up beside hers. "Hmm, this won't work either." He slid the chair to face her and reached for her hands.

"Oh, Jordan. You're going to pull me out of the chair."

"Maybe, but if I do, you'll fall on me. Would that be so bad?"

He pulled her closer, leaned in, making sure she didn't slip out of the chair and touched her lips softly. "See, we just have to make adjustments."

"Maybe, but you scared me to death," Jessie said.

"Love, your racing heart was the effect of my kiss, not fear," he joked and kissed her again.

"Right." Jessie gave him a little push. "You're a nut."

"Uh, huh. Nutty about you." Jordan glanced around the room. "Would you like to take a walk and get out of here for a bit?'

Jessie gave him a look.

"Oh, yeah, sorry. You roll. I'll walk."

Jordan walked beside Jessie as she maneuvered her wheelchair. They roamed the halls for a while and ended up in the cafe. The hot lunch line wasn't open yet, but there were cold items to purchase. "Let's get something and sit here for a while," Jordan said.

Jordan's eyes lit up as they ate their sandwiches, "I almost forgot to tell you something. You know Vikki's sister, Mary, and her boyfriend, Robbie?" Jessie nodded. "Well, Robbie's band is planning to hold a benefit concert at the church to raise money to help remodel my house and make it wheelchair accessible for you." Jordan smiled broadly. "They are widening the doors, taking up the carpet, lowering counters, everything. Isn't that great?"

Jessie's face clouded. "Oh, I haven't even thought about that. Yes, Yes, it's a wonderful thing to do, but.." she bit her lower lip. "It's just…"

"What, Love? What's wrong?"

Jessie squeezed her fingers together. "It's just, well, my parents, especially my mother, plan on me moving in with them for a while."

Jordan's stomach flipped. "What gave them that idea? He reached for her hands across the table. "I know we missed our wedding date, but we'll get married as soon as you're released."

Jessie hesitated as if she wasn't sure what to say. "Jordan, maybe we should delay getting married. It will give us both time to adjust."

Jordan's heart thudded against his chest. "Jessie, what do you mean? We can adjust together. I know your mom wants to protect you, but that's my place now. It's not her decision." He tightened his grip on her hands, but she pulled them away.

"Jordan, think about it for a minute. I am going to need a lot of help while I learn how to care for myself."

His expression stiffened. "Jessie, I know that, and I can be the one to help."

"But I may need others to help when you're not home."

Jordan took a deep breath and struggled to keep his voice calm. "If you need more help, we'll deal with that," he said with clipped words. "Jessie, I won't let your parents dictate what we do."

Jessie's eyes flashed. "Jordan, be reasonable. My

parents want to help, that's all. We need to consider what they say."

Jordan's head was swimming. He hadn't seen this coming, but he guessed he should have, knowing Marianne. "I am trying to be reasonable, but this idea of you moving in with your parents has thrown me for a loop. I can take care of you."

Jessie's expression softened, and she slipped her hands back into his. "Jordan, I have to learn to catheterize myself. Did you know that? And there is something called a bowel program. The nurses have been doing these things for me, and soon they will teach me how to do them myself. But I might need help for some time."

The irritation drained from Jordan. She seemed so vulnerable, so unsure of her future. "I know, Love. I've had enough medical training to know at least some of it. And I've done a little research around here." He caressed her thumb. "I understand the procedures, and I can help you with them if needed."

Jessie peered at him. "But it's not just that." A tear formed in the corner of her eye and trickled down her cheek. "What about our physical relationship? I — I'm paralyzed from the waist down."

Jordan flinched at the anguish in her eyes. He spun her wheelchair around and took both her hands. "Jessie, I want to be with you as your husband. We'll figure it out. I love you for you. Just holding you next to me is all I long for right now."

Jessie studied his face. "But Jordan, you've waited for marriage. It doesn't seem right to have someone who can't— "

"Don't say it." Jordan put two fingers on her mouth. "Don't ever think you won't be enough." He brought her hands to his lips. "Please don't sell me short. I love you. I want to be with you. Like I said, we'll figure it out."

Silence settled over them as Jessie's gaze fell from his. It was nearing lunchtime, and people began gathering in the cafe. A few patients were at their assistant's mercy, who attended to their every need. Others navigated the room with their wheelchair or walker like it was as ordinary as another person walking. Some wore expressions of fear or despair, while others seemed confident and at ease. Jordan followed Jessie's gaze, surveying the scene.

She held his eyes for a long moment. "I'm one of them now, Jordan."

"Let's go and get you back in your bed. I think you need to rest," Jordan said with a hoarse whisper.

Jordan's temples pounded, and he was sure Jessie was exhausted. When they returned to the room, Jessie agreed that she needed to lie down. He positioned the board the way he'd seen the nurses do it, helped Jessie transfer back into her bed, and tucked the blanket around her.

"Let's talk about all this later." Jordan kissed her cheek. "I have to work my shift, but I'll be back in a couple of days. I'll call you tomorrow. Get some rest now so you will be ready for your next therapy session."

Jessie nodded. "I will. We both need time to process everything." She smiled a little. "Oh, by the way, thanks for the teddy bear." She pointed to the table that held the vase with the bear and the angel.

"I didn't send you that bear."

"Oh." Jessie frowned. "It had no name, so I thought you sent it to tease me about my love of stuffed bears."

"No, but I wish I had thought about doing that. I guess you'll have to ask around."

"I guess. Bye, Jordan. Call me."

"I will. Goodbye, Love." He gave her fingers a gentle squeeze and then walked out the door.

* * *

Jeremy sighed as he watched Jordan pull into the fire station. He had gotten there early and already attended to his shift duties. If it was a quiet night, he hoped to have time to talk with Jordan.

Jordan greeted him with his usual, "Hey, Preacher Boy," but his smile didn't quite reach his eyes. Jeremy understood the worry on Jordan's face. He was on edge himself knowing his sister's life had changed forever. It must be excruciating for his friend.

"Hi, Jordan. How was Jessie today?"

"Okay, I guess. We took a walk to the cafeteria. She's trying to get used to everything."

"I'm sure that will take some time, but she's strong." Jeremy motioned for Jordan to join him at the table. "Did you tell Jessie about the plans to remodel your house?"

Jordan's eyes shadowed. "Yes." He gave Jeremy a probing look. "Do you know anything about your parents wanting Jessie to move in with them when she gets out of the rehab center?"

Jeremy sat on the couch in the firehouse lounge. Jordan's expression told him that he wasn't pleased with the proposal. "Yes. As a matter of fact, I was planning to bring that up to you today. I didn't know that Jessie had told you."

"It came up."

"I see. Listen, Jordan. They are trying to do what they think is best for Jessie. It isn't about anything else."

Jordan took a seat facing Jeremy and smirked. "Protect her from me, you mean. They think that I won't be able to handle all the care Jessie will need and that I'll bail on her."

Jeremy met Jordan's stare. His friend never minced words. But he needed to understand that it was more complicated than he assumed. "Jordan, you know my parents adore you. They think you are a godsend for their strong-willed daughter. But my mom is super protective of her children." He grunted. "Believe me, I've experienced it."

Jordan gripped the arms of the chair. "Yeah, I know. They will cater to her every need, your mom especially. She won't let Jessie reach her full potential. She'll shelter her too much. I'll be able to help her be more independent."

"That's not fair, Jordan. This is difficult for all of us." Jeremy pushed his bangs across his forehead. "Anyway, Mom and Dad want you and me to come for dinner when we get off our shift while Vikki visits Jessie. Will you come and at least listen to what they have to say?"

Jordan's eyes lifted. "I'll come and listen, but I won't be silent."

"That's all I'm asking."

CHAPTER FOUR

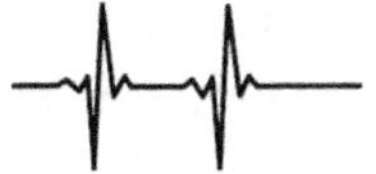

"Hi, come on in. Dinner will be ready as soon as you wash up."

Jeremy greeted his mom with a hug. "It smells wonderful."

Marianne smiled at Jordan. "We're so glad you could make it. I made lasagna," she said. "I remember how much you liked it."

Jordan breathed in the delicious aroma of Italian spices. "Mmm, lasagna. Yours is the best I've ever had." He turned to Frank and shook his hand. "How are you doing, Sir?"

Everyone enjoyed the mouthwatering entree for a few minutes and engaged in casual chatter. Jordan felt Marianne's eyes on him and wondered when the conversation would turn to the subject that he knew prompted the dinner invitation. His answer came over dessert.

"I know you love cherry pie," Marianne said as she brought the nicely browned pie to the table. "Do you remember I served it when Jessie brought you home to meet us?"

"Oh yes, lasagna and cherry pie," he replied with a touch of sarcasm. "I think I'm being set up."

Marianne's eyes snapped. "Would you care for some tonight, or not?"

"Sure." Jordan smothered a grin. It was apparent where Jessie got her spunk.

A tense quiet fell over the room. Frank cleared his throat. "Jordan, Marianne and I know how much you care for our daughter, but we think it would be best for her to move in with us after she's released from the hospital." He paused for a second. "Just for a while."

Jordan stiffened at Frank's matter-of-fact tone and felt his jaw twitch. "That's not happening."

"Frank's right," Marianne said. "Jessie will feel more comfortable in her home while she adjusts to her new circumstances." She tapped her fingers on the table. "Jordan, she is going to need assistance with her personal needs. You shouldn't be the one helping her."

Jordan kept his voice steady. "Marianne, I know the extent of Jessie's injuries and understand what kind of help she'll need, and I'm willing to give it to her. We plan to be married as soon as she's released." He scrunched his eyebrows, "She has her own apartment, anyway. She doesn't live here."

"Come on, Jordan, you know what I mean." Marianne's voice raised a notch. "Jessie needs to be here with us— at least for now. She doesn't need more changes. And do you plan to help her with her catheter and bowel program? Do you think either of you will feel comfortable with that?" She cast him a look that said she had stated the obvious. "Well, do you?"

"Probably more comfortable than you'd be. You

strike me as someone who might find that a little too gritty." Jordan caught Jeremy's amazed stare and gave him an eye shrug.

Marianne flushed. "You don't know what I'm capable of, and if needed, we could hire help." Her eyes were stony, but her voice held a tremble. "And what about your job? You're away from home two or three nights a week. Who will help Jessie, then?"

"We can work around that. Hire a caregiver when needed. And some of Jessie's friends might be willing to help." Jordan relaxed his fists. "Frank and Marianne, I know you want what's best for your daughter, but if Jessie and I were already married would we be having this conversation?"

Frank raised his chin. "Of course not, Jordan. But that's not the situation we have now."

"No," Marianne said. "No, it's not. Think about it, Jordan. We're concerned about you, too. You'll be Jessie's caregiver forever, and your life as a young man will change drastically. Right now, you have other choices." She paused and lowered her voice. "You need to think about that."

Jordan's features tightened, and he opened his mouth to tell her he didn't need to consider other choices, but Frank spoke first.

"Jordan, we're not asking you to step out of Jessie's life. We just want you to think about things, maybe wait for a while before you make a marriage commitment. Have you prayed about it?"

Jordan's face grew warm, and he lifted his chin. "I don't need to pray about it." He met Frank's probing eyes. "I mean, of course I've prayed for Jessie. But her accident changes nothing about my intentions to marry her. I know what I'm getting into."

Marianne crossed her arms. "What do your parents say about all this?"

Jordan slid his chair from the table and shot to his feet. "Believe it or not, they have faith in me. They know I'm capable of making decisions that affect my life. You say I have choices, but you don't mean that. You're afraid, and I can understand that, but don't try to control me. I don't need your approval, but I'd appreciate your support."

Jeremy tossed Jordan a warning look. "Hey everyone, let's calm down. All of us want what's best for Jessie. A decision doesn't have to be made tonight." He placed his palms on the table and took a deep breath. "Anyway, all this is Jessie's decision. Don't you think so?"

Jordan dropped into his seat and met Marianne's eyes. "Jeremy's right." His eyes shadowed. "Jessie will make the ultimate decision. She's the one most affected." The quiet tension returned as the truth of the moment echoed around the table.

* * *

"How do you think dinner is going with your parents and Jordan?" Vikki asked as she wheeled Jessie down the hall following a quiet dinner in the cafe. "Jeremy told me your parents want Jordan to agree to you moving in with them for a while after you're released from here."

She paused for a second and then continued. "He doesn't think Jordan will go for that plan."

Jessie sighed. "That's an understatement. I've already brought it up to him, and he's definitely not on board."

Vikki pushed Jessie through the door and positioned a chair in front of her. Her green eyes looked thoughtful. "What do you want, Jessie?"

"Funny, you're the first person to ask me. Everyone is busy trying to figure out my life." Her lower lip quivered. "They don't seem to care what I want."

"Tell me. I'll listen."

Jessie looked at the woman who had brought her brother back to life and had become her best friend. She trusted her quiet solidness. "I really don't know, Vikki. I can't think beyond today. I'm just holding on by a thread."

"Don't you think you have a right to feel vulnerable?"

Jessie's eyes filled. She hadn't let anyone see her cry since the doctor told her about her paralysis, but Vikki's simple question caused a flood of tears. "I'm sorry." she sobbed.

Vikki found some tissues and handed them to her. She sat and put her hand on Jessie's knee. "It's okay to cry, Jessie. It's okay to feel helpless and afraid."

Jessie blew her nose. "Thank you, Vikki. Thank you for understanding. Everyone tells me how strong I am, how I'm a fighter. But it's not true. Right now, I'm fragile and barely able to function— let alone fight."

Vikki patted her shoulder. "It's alright not to be strong. God will help you find that strength again. Right now, you're broken, but you'll rise again."

"I don't know if I can. I'm tired and frightened about all this. I know God is with me, but I don't feel his presence."

"You're fine, Jessie. God doesn't depend on our awareness for Him to be present, but maybe His desire is for you to lay your fear and anger before Him."

"Thanks, Vikki. It helps to be reminded of that." She wiped away her tears. "And I don't know what to do about Jordan. I love him, but I don't want him to have to care for me all his life."

"Don't you think Jordan's willing to care for you?"

"Yes, but he has too much integrity to leave. I don't want him to feel forced to marry me."

"I don't think your injuries cause him to doubt. He loves you and wants to be with you."

"That's what he says, but my parents don't think he's considering all the aspects of my care. I don't question Jordan's love for me, but I'm not sure he's seeing the big picture either."

Jessie swiped at another tear. "To tell you the truth, I don't want to think about it. I'd rather live in denial right now, 'cause I don't want to face this," she said with a wobbly smile.

Vikki's eyes brimmed with tears. "You don't have to think about it now. Just work on getting through today, and let things mellow out a little. You have time."

Jessie squeezed Vikki's hand. "You're right about that. I'll be here for a while."

"Yes. Just take it a day at a time." Vikki sniffed and hugged Jessie's shoulders. "I'll see you later. I'll pray for your wisdom and strength."

Jessie smiled at her friend, knowing Vikki's words were more than good intentions. "Thank you. I treasure your prayers."

As Vikki turned to leave, her eyes fell on a new little brown bear sitting on a table in Jessie's room. "Oh, how sweet. Jordan's going all out with the Teddy Bear joke."

Jessie shook her head. "They aren't from him. I have no idea who sent them. This one just appeared outside my door like the last one."

"Strange," Vikki said, "Maybe it's someone from church."

* * *

Jeremy was silent as he drove Jordan home after the dinner with his parents which was fine with Jordan. He didn't want to hear any more about the after dinner discussion. But when Jeremy pulled into Jordan's driveway, he sat with both hands on the wheel and looked straight ahead.

"Wait a minute before you get out. I need to say something."

Jordan bristled. "Say it."

"Jordan, I know you love my sister and believe you can handle meeting all her physical needs. I don't doubt that at all." Jeremy turned toward him, "But have you considered the emotional effects? I mean for both of you?"

Jordan frowned and narrowed his eyes. "Of course, I've thought about that. I know Jessie is upset and afraid, but I can handle that. I can help her through it."

"Jordan, she's devastated, not just upset. Don't you see that? And what about you?"

"What are you talking about? I am not the one who's hurt," Jordan said with a tinge of scorn. "Listen, Jeremy, I have thought about what it means to take care of Jessie's needs. I understand that it will be a huge adjustment for both of us, but it's one I'm willing to make."

Jeremy rubbed his forehead. "Jordan, you can't conquer this with grit. Your mind knows the severity of the situation, but I'm not sure your heart believes it."

Jordan felt his fingers tightened. "What do you want me to do? Desert Jessie because of her injuries? What kind of man would I be if I did that?"

"No, I don't want you to desert Jessie. I want you by her side forever, but not out of a feeling of obligation. And not because you want to be a hero." He paused and lowered his voice. "Jessie wouldn't want that, and neither would you. That sense of duty can lead to resentment. I just want you to take a hard look at the reality of the situation. Pray about it."

Jordan's mouth gaped. Jeremy had never called him out or challenged his motives before. His tone lost its edginess. "I'm no hero. I love Jessie. I want to be with her. God knows I've prayed."

"I believe you, Jordan. I just want you to go into this for the right reasons."

"I am." Jordan struggled for control. "I can't fix this for Jessie. I hate that." He struck the dashboard. "I have no right to be angry, but I am." He met Jeremy's gaze. "You understand that don't you?"

Jeremy nodded. "You know I do. After Shannon's death, I pushed the rage deep inside my soul because the intensity of it scared me, so it's good you own it. It's okay to be angry as long as you don't let it control you. It took me years and Brandon's encouragement to face my resentment." He smiled a little. "You're right. You can't fix this. I guess I just needed to hear you say it."

* * *

Jeremy's words replayed in Jordan's mind the following morning as he drove to the mechanic's shop for another visit. He must commit to Jessie out of love, not out of a self-righteous feeling of responsibility. He wanted to marry Jessie, though. He knew that for sure. He pulled into the parking lot.

Jordan had requested Jessie's car be towed to the shop that had changed her tires right before she had the accident on her way to Claymon. Amber led Jordan to Jessie's crumpled red car sitting in the back lot. He shuddered at the sight of it and wondered how Jessie had survived.

Amber assured him her lead mechanic checked everything out but could not determine what had made the wheel fall off. She said her technicians always followed strict safety rules when working on car tires and insisted that the lug bolts could have been defective.

Jordan sensed Amber was protecting her crew but had almost decided to let it drop. He had no proof of anything. As they were walking back to the shop, he caught the eye of someone watching them from the open garage. The young man held Jordan's gaze for a beat, then disappeared behind a car. Jordan had seen the guy somewhere before but couldn't place him. He must be one of the mechanics, but why was he watching him like that?

CHAPTER FIVE

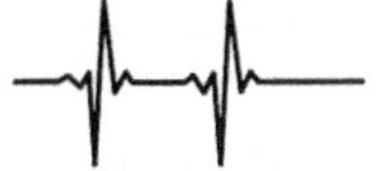

Jordan walked through the doors of New Life Community Church. Brandon was preaching today, so he found Jeremy and Vikki sitting toward the back of the sanctuary.

"Hey, how's it going?" Jeremy asked, scooting down a seat. "Are you still speaking to me?"

"Yeah. I guess I needed to hear what you had to say. You sure were in your element last night, Preacher Boy."

"What do you mean by that?"

"Oh, come on." He leaned forward a little to get Vikki's attention. "Did Jeremy tell you he sat quietly as a mouse during that whole discussion at his parents' house and then shamed us all with his words of wisdom?"

Vikki's lips rose in a smile. "He mentioned something about it."

"Well, then when he dropped me off, Preacher Boy here," he gave Jeremy a nudge, "gave me a little sermon about having a hero complex. He can't help it, though. It's in his blood."

Vikki giggled, and Jeremy laughed out loud.

"Shh! Cut it out guys," Jordan said as if shocked at their behavior, "The service is starting. Don't embarrass me." He sat back in his seat and gave Brandon's wife, Alice, who had turned around at the sound of laughter, an eye roll and whispered, "Some people just don't know how to behave in church. Poor upbringing, I guess." Alice looked at Jeremy and giggled before returning her attention to the service.

Jordan enjoyed Brandon's teaching almost as much as Jeremy's. Their styles differed, with Jeremy being more casual in his presentation, but both delivered thought-provoking messages. Today was no different. Brandon's sermon this morning about the importance of having pure motives for all of one's actions and not doing good works for the sake of others' praise amazed Jordan. Had he been the subject of some late night chat between Jeremy and Brandon? He stole a sideways glance at his friend. Jeremy looked at him and shrugged.

After the service, a young man hanging out in the foyer with a group of teens caught Jordan's eye. It was the employee who'd watched him from behind the car at the mechanic's shop. Now he knew why the guy had looked familiar. He'd attended the youth meeting once or twice. The kid noticed Jordan and cut away from his group of friends. Jordan lost sight of him as he tried to maneuver through the crowd but caught a glimpse of the teen as he bolted through the church doors. Jordan stood in the doorway and scrunched his brow as the young man rushed down the sidewalk.

"Where did you take off to so fast?" Jeremy asked as he approached Jordan.

"I recognized someone I needed to talk to. Wait a second, I'll be right back."

Jordan ambled over to the group of teens standing near the welcome desk. "Hi, guys."

"Hi, Jordan. How's Jessie?" a young teenage boy asked. "I heard she's paralyzed."

A girl elbowed him. "We're so sorry, Jordan." She glared at the boy who had asked about Jessie. "We all miss you guys."

The teens nodded and murmured their concern for Jessie. Jordan smiled at the boy who had greeted him first. "It's okay to ask. Yes, she is paralyzed from the waist down. She will have to be in a wheelchair, but she'll be okay. I'll tell Jessie you asked about her. That will make her happy." He turned to the girl who had elbowed the teen boy. "By the way, who is the kid with long hair that was hanging with you guys a few minutes ago? I know I've seen him at youth group before, but I can't remember his name."

"His name's Aiden. He came to the youth group with Nick a couple of times, but he just showed up here by himself today."

"Oh, I see. I think I saw him at Claymon's Mechanic Shop the other day."

"Yeah, he works there," another youth said. "So, when are you coming back to the youth group meetings?"

"I'm not sure. Between work and visiting Jessie, I'm pretty busy, but I'll try to stop by soon."

"Do you think we could visit Jessie?"

Jordan hesitated. Seeing the kids might lift her spirits. "I'll tell you what. She is pretty weak right now, but give her a little bit, and I'm sure she would like to see all of you. When she's stronger, the church is planning a benefit for her with Robbie's band playing the music. Maybe you could come to that."

"Cool, that's the band that played for Pastor Jeremy's wedding, right?"

"Yep, the very one."

* * *

Aiden buried his head in his hands as he sat in the well-worn seat of his faded blue Malibu. Why had he come to church today? It wasn't something he'd planned, but somehow, he felt compelled to be there. He should have known Jordan would spot him.

He'd heard about Jessie's accident the day after it happened and made the connection during the youth group when Pastor Jeremy explained why Jessie and Jordan weren't there. He remembered the kids admiring Jessie's Mustang the first time he'd come to the group.

When Amber questioned each of the mechanics after Jordan's first visit to the shop, Aiden had let Amber believe he'd finished the job. It wasn't a lie, not really. He just let her assume he had tightened the lug nuts. But he hadn't, and now a woman was paralyzed. Even worse, she was someone he knew. Aiden closed his eyes as the events of that fateful morning replayed in his head.

It was his fourth week working in Amber's shop. Randy was overseeing him complete a tire change on a red Mustang when Amber called Randy to the front desk to help a customer.

"Go ahead and finish tightening the lug nuts on the front tires. I'll be back in a minute," Randy said.

Aiden carefully tightened the left front tire and then moved to the one on the right. His phone rang, and he pulled it out of his pocket, intending to silence it, until he noticed it was a call from his father and answered it. His father had fallen. He jogged to the front of the shop.

"My father fell again, and he needs my help."

"Sure, go to him," Amber urged, "Do you need someone to go with you?"

"No, I can help him up and get him settled into his wheelchair. It won't take too long."

"Take your time."

"Thanks, I'll be back."

On the drive back to the shop after helping his father, Aiden thought about the Mustang. *I didn't tighten the lug nuts on the last tire. But, of course, Randy would finish the job. He always checked the newer mechanic's work. But apparently, he hadn't.*

When Aiden returned to work, he noticed the Mustang was gone. He looked for Randy, but he'd left early. Aiden assumed Randy had tightened the lug nuts on the last wheel until he heard about the wreck.

The sound of car doors opening roused Aiden from his memories. He turned over his engine and pulled away. Did Amber know the truth? If so, why hadn't she confronted him? Jordan must have recognized him as the person watching from behind the car when he came to the shop the other day and probably suspected he was the one responsible for Jessie's injuries.

Aiden realized he was lucky Amber had given him a chance when he applied at the shop. An eighteen-year-old dropout usually didn't get hired as a mechanic. But he had assured her he was taking classes online to finish school and was a quick learner with basic mechanical skills. His father, who had once been a good mechanic, had taught him how to work on cars.

But that was long before everything fell apart— before the accident ended his mother's life, before his father's diagnosis of Multiple Sclerosis two years later. As Aiden turned the car onto the street, he reached across the seat to keep his purchase from falling on the floorboard.

* * *

After church, Jordan drove to the rehab center, glad to be off shift until Tuesday. Saturday after work had been spent at Frank and Marianne's ill-fated dinner party, but now he would have a couple of days to be with Jessie. Marianne had probably skipped church and spent the morning with her daughter. He was thankful Jessie's parents were attentive since he worked a firefighter's schedule, but he hoped to spend some time alone with her. He walked toward the revolving hospital door. A person stepped out as he entered. It was that kid, Aiden, he'd seen at church.

"Hey, wait up!" Jordan called, pushing through the door until he was outside again. A look of recognition flashed in Aiden's eyes, and he turned away, quickening his pace.

Jordan knew he could overtake the teen easily but stayed a few feet behind. "Aiden, stop for a minute. Please, I need to talk to you."

Aiden spun around to face Jordan. "What do you want?" he demanded.

Jordan approached him with unhurried steps. "I'm Jordan. Do you remember me from church? I saw you there today and tried to get your attention, but you left in a hurry."

"Uh, I guess I didn't see you," Aiden crossed his arms and looked at the ground. "I have to go, now."

Jordan inched closer. "Were you visiting someone here?"

"Um, no, I, uh, I was delivering food. Yeah, I'm a pizza delivery guy."

"I see," Jordan said, scanning Aiden for any sign that he was on the level. "I thought I saw you at Claymon's Mechanic Shop the other day. The kids at church said you worked there."

Aiden stared at the pavement. "Uh, right, I work there, too, but…" his voice faded, then grew defiant, "I don't remember ever seeing you. I gotta go now."

Jordan decided to let him off the hook. He shrugged. "Okay, see you around." Aiden hurried away and looked back at Jordan before he opened the car door. Jordan stood in the parking lot as Aiden drove away. That kid was trying awfully hard to avoid him. What was he hiding?

Jordan walked the long hallway to the turn leading to Jessie's room. Marianne was rearranging items on the bedside table that held Jessie's TV remote, phone, and a variety of other objects.

Jessie's eyes lit up when he entered the room. "Hi, I thought you'd be here about now."

"Hi, Love." He nodded to Jessie's mother, "Hello, Marianne."

She lifted her head but didn't meet his eyes. "Hello, Jordan."

The dark circles under Marianne's eyes gave Jordan a twinge of guilt. She must be bone-tired from worry and lack of sleep. "Have you guys eaten yet? We could go to the cafeteria and get something."

Marianne moved from the bedside table to the closet. "You two go ahead. I think I'll stay here and straighten the closet a little."

Jordan walked over to her. "Marianne, you look worn out. Come with us and get some lunch."

Marianne hesitated, and Jessie spoke up, "Come on, Mom. You need to eat something."

The trio silently headed to the cafe and joined the serving line. Marianne stiffened, drawing Jordan's attention to the day's entree.

He snickered at the steaming tray of lasagna, "It's okay, Marianne. At least there's no cherry pie. I think we're safe."

Marianne tossed Jordan a scathing look and chose a chef salad instead of the hot meal. Jessie looked from her mom to Jordan with questioning eyes.

"It's an inside joke, Love. I'll explain later," he mumbled, helping guide her through the crowd as she held her food tray.

Jordan caught up on Jessie's past few days while they ate. He glanced at Marianne, who seemed absorbed with her salad.

"Don't worry, Marianne," Jordan said, pointing to his plate of lasagna, "It isn't nearly as delicious as yours."

Marianne cracked a snide smile, "Well, that's good. I guess you are safe then."

Jordan chuckled for a second then grew serious. "Marianne, I appreciate all the time you spend with Jessie and know you must be exhausted. I'm sorry about my attitude last night."

Marianne looked at him with tired eyes. "We were all on edge, I think. I told Jessie about our conversation," she said eyeing her daughter, "I'm sure she will make the choice that will be best for everyone."

Jordan took in her meaningful glance toward Jessie. Marianne would be a formidable adversary if he didn't stay in her good graces. "I'm sure that's true. Luckily, you and Frank have raised a strong, independent woman."

Jessie sat up straighter and squared her shoulders. Her eyes flashed. "If you two don't mind, Jeremy's right. It is my decision, and I don't have the energy to make those choices right now. I need both of you to stop pressuring me."

Jordan lowered his eyes. It was her decision, but it terrified him. "I'm sorry, Jessie. Right now, we just need to work on getting you stronger."

Marianne nodded her agreement with a determined smile. "Yes, Jessie. You have plenty of time to think about what you need to do."

After lunch, Marianne consented to go home and rest, leaving Jordan to spend the afternoon with Jessie. She had a physical therapy class scheduled at 2:00, and Jordan asked to attend since he would be Jessie's caregiver.

As Becky performed a series of range of motion exercises on Jessie's legs, she explained that the knee bends, stretches, and leg lifts would promote circulation and prevent muscle atrophy. Jordan nodded and asked if she would teach him how to perform the exercises.

"Sure," Becky replied. "It's good for you to learn. As Jessie gets stronger, she will take over the arm exercises herself, but she'll need someone to stretch her legs."

For the next half hour, Becky taught Jordan how to execute each movement, and though it felt awkward at first, he mastered each one by the end of the session.

"That wasn't so bad," Jordan said after completing the exercise series. "How often should these be done?"

"Ideally, every day," Becky replied. "But as I said, Jessie will be able to help with them as soon as she gains strength."

"Every day?" Jessie said.

"Oh, I won't mind that at all. I've always kinda liked

your legs," Jordan said with a wink to Jessie, who rewarded him with a swat on his arm.

Becky laughed, "At any rate, these exercises will be beneficial in keeping Jessie's leg muscles strong and improving her circulation."

After the physical therapy session, Jessie guided them to a cozy room with floor-to-ceiling windows that ushered in a sunny blue-skyed afternoon. A reclining couch and a couple of chairs sat against one wall.

"There's usually not a lot of people here. Do you want to stay and talk for a while?"

"Sure, it seems peaceful."

Jessie nodded, "Yes, it's a good place to come and meditate." She looked up at Jordan. "I have a break until the evening before my next therapy session. I have to practice transferring from my chair to my bed and back before my shower."

"Wow, they give you a workout here, don't they?" Jordan asked as he lowered himself into a cushioned chair next to Jessie.

"Yes, but it's lighter on the weekend. During the week, I have at least three sessions a day. It seems like everything I once knew how to do, I have to learn again."

Jordan took her hand and caressed her fingers. "I'm sure it seems overwhelming now, but I know my strong and spunky girl. You'll master all those things, and one day they will seem normal to you."

Jessie looked at him with sad looking eyes. "Jordan, I'm not that strong. I feel helpless and so…so confused about everything, and…and I— I don't want to go through this." She brushed her tears with her sleeve. "I want my life back."

"Aw, Jessie," Jordan said and offered her a Kleenex

from a box on a nearby table, "I know you do." He had no words of comfort, but there was something he could do that might help. He wheeled her over to the couch.

"What are you doing, Jordan?"

"We are going to transfer you to this couch, Love. You're going to need to help just a bit."

"But Jordan, we can't— "

"Oh, yes we can," he said with a sassy smile. "If you put your hand on the couch and lean over, I can swivel you on to it."

Jordan held onto Jessie's hips and helped her slide onto the couch. After making sure she was steady, he sat down and wrapped his arm around her. She snuggled closer and laid her head on his shoulder.

Jordan leaned over and kissed her cheek. "I've wanted to hold you like this for a long time."

Jessie looked up at him with a flicker of a smile. "It is good to be out of the chair and be next to you."

Jordan knew what would make this even better. "You need a footstool." He positioned the wheelchair facing the couch and placed Jessie's legs on it. Then he hopped back on the sofa and raised his footrest.

"There now, we're all set." Jordan lifted her chin so that his eyes peered into hers. "I can't give you your old life back, Love, but I can be a part of the life you have now. You're still the same person. You'll always be the beautiful girl I fell in love with."

"But I'm not, Jordan, I'm not the same."

Jordan sighed and drew her closer until she rested her head on his shoulder. He grabbed the blanket from the armrest and leaned back, holding the curve of Jessie's body next to him. He closed his eyes and breathed in the sweet scent of her hair softly grazing the side of his face. His eyes opened at approaching footsteps.

"Well, you guys look all cozy," Jeremy teased with lifted eyebrows. "I'm not even going to ask how Jessie got on that couch with you, although I'm sure some rules were broken in the process."

Jessie sat up and let out a little laugh. "What do you think, Jeremy? Jordan just picked me up and tossed me."

Vikki smiled. "Somehow I believe that."

"Oh no, she helped," Jordan said, patting Jessie's arm. "She's becoming an expert at transferring."

After a few minutes, Jeremy offered to help Jordan work on his house while Vikki visited with Jessie. "You said something about laying new tile in the bathroom."

Jordan nodded, "Sure, that would work if it's okay with Jessie."

"I think that's a good idea. I know Jordan could use the help."

Jordan assisted Jessie as she slid back in her chair with only a slight wobbling. "See, that was pretty smooth. You'll be a pro soon." He knelt by the wheelchair and lifted Jessie's chin. Twisting a curl around his finger, he whispered, "Bye, Love." He squeezed her hand and caught Vikki's eye. "I think she could use some girl talk."

CHAPTER SIX

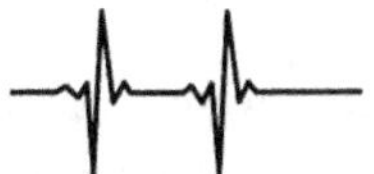

"So, how has your day been, Jessie?" Vikki asked after Jordan and Jeremy left.

"Fine, I guess, I'm just learning to manage the therapy sessions and this wheelchair."

"I'm sure that's draining, both physically and emotionally."

Jessie smiled at her friend. Vikki always seemed to understand, and she rarely offered unsolicited advice. "I could use a soda. Do you want to go to the cafe?'

"Sure, lead the way."

The girls took their drinks to a small table. "Oh, by the way," Vikki said as she sipped her soda, "a couple of ladies from church said they might visit you this afternoon."

"Which ones?" Jessie asked.

"Brandon's wife Alice, and Diane. Maybe Lilly."

"Diane is Patrick's wife, right? I don't believe I know Lilly."

Vikki frowned. "Yes, and Lilly is her friend. She's almost as bad as Diane."

Jessie's eyes danced. "Why Vikki, I've never heard you criticize anyone. What's the matter with Diane?"

Vikki's cheeks flushed. "Oh, Diane thinks it's pretty special being an elder's wife, I guess. She isn't too fond of me, and Patrick has never liked Jeremy." She paused briefly, "Patrick and Lee Bannister were good friends."

Jessie shuddered at the sound of Lee's name. She knew her encounter with him several years earlier was partly to blame for his scornful attitude toward Jeremy. God's grace had performed its miracle in her soul, but sometimes in moments of uncertainty, memories, especially the most secret one lurking in the recesses of her mind, threatened to drown her with guilt. She shoved the accusing thoughts aside. "How could Patrick defend Lee? He served time for beating his wife and attacking us after you let Brandon know about his abusive behavior."

Vikki lifted her shoulders. "I don't know. I guess Patrick believes Lee got a raw deal, losing his partnership in his father in law's practice. Anyway, when Lee served as an elder, he and Patrick didn't approve of Jeremy's appointment as associate pastor, and that was before Lee realized you were Jeremy's sister. Patrick and his cronies don't like Jeremy's way of challenging the congregation to grow in their walk with the Lord. You know, live like Christians. They see church membership as an advantage for their professional careers and opportunities for connections in the community, so they want New Life Community to be a prestigious church instead of one after the heart of God. Those people aren't interested in discipleship. Jeremy hates that attitude."

She set down her can with a clunk. "Yet, they put on

this facade of holiness. Patrick even gave Jeremy grief because Robbie's band played some secular dance music at our wedding."

"You've got to be kidding," Jessie said. "Nothing they played was inappropriate."

"I know. It's absurd. Brandon approves of Jeremy's teaching, though. You can see the shift in some of his own sermons. That doesn't sit well with Patrick at all."

"Well, it should be an interesting visit then, don't you think? Why do they want to visit me anyway?"

"Oh, I'm sure Diane thinks it's her duty." Vikki touched the cross on her necklace. "I'm sorry. I'm sure they do want to see you, especially Alice. I shouldn't talk that way about them. I'm a little too sensitive, I guess."

Jessie doubted Vikki's self assessment. She'd sensed the same feeling of judgment the few times she'd spoken with Diane. "Well, we should probably head back toward my room. Maybe I can freshen up a bit before they get here. I don't want to scare them to death."

As they neared Jessie's room, voices wafted out into the hallway. "Wait, listen," Jessie whispered and held up her hand.

"What do you mean, Jordan's a saint?"

"Well, Patrick told me things about Jessie that would shock you," Diane lowered her voice, "I can't tell anyone, of course. Let's just say Jessie might not be the good Christian girl you think she is, if you know what I mean. Anyway, I say he's a saint because he's willing to marry her even after the accident left her paralyzed. He'll have to take care of her forever. And what can she do? Not much of anything except sit there. It will be his cross to bear, I guess."

Jessie's pulse hammered against her temples, and she

looked back at Vikki, whose face was ashen. Vikki started to pull the chair away.

Jessie shook her head and mouthed, "Stay here."

Alice's voice came next. "Diane don't talk like that. Jordan loves Jessie. I'm sure he's willing to care for her. And she's still the same person. She just can't walk, that's all."

"Come on, Alice. We don't live in a fairy tale world. He may love her, but he'll soon regret marrying her. When the guys are out having fun, he'll be stuck at home with her. He's a young man and what about, well you know... the bedroom? Can people like Jessie even..."

Jessie lunged into the room at that instant, dragging an astonished Vikki behind her. She put on the sweetest smile she could manage, "Well, hello. I didn't expect company."

The three women gawked at Jessie until Alice stammered, "Oh, uh, a nurse told us we could wait here for you."

"I'm so pleased you came to visit."

Vikki cleared her throat. "Hi, ladies. Why don't we all sit down?" Her green eyes snapped. "Instead of huddling at the door."

"Oh, I didn't see you, Vikki," Diane said as they pulled chairs around, "Come to think of it, I don't remember seeing you at church this morning either."

"I wasn't hiding."

Diane's lips curled up. "Honey, if you stood by in the greeting line, it would show you supported your husband."

"Is that right? I didn't know I was permanently attached to Jeremy, and he didn't even give the sermon this morning."

Diane stepped closer. "Perhaps Jeremy needs to teach you proper etiquette for a preacher's wife."

Vikki lifted her chin, "Actually, I'm Jeremy's partner, not his student."

"Leave her alone, Diane," Alice said, "She's doing a fine job as a preacher's wife."

Jessie covered her mouth. Wow! What just happened? She'd never heard Vikki speak to anyone with that tone. "Well, here we are," she burst out. Lilly gulped as Jessie offered her hand. "By the way, I'm Jessie. Glad to meet you."

After a few awkward seconds, Alice coughed and glanced at her companions. "Jessie, we just wanted to stop in for a minute and see how you were doing." Her eyes swept the room, "This seems like a nice place to recover. It's clean and I bet the staff is— is helpful." She gave Jessie a weak smile.

"It's a great place. All the professionals here teach us to see ourselves as more than disabled beings taking up space with our wheelchairs." She glared at Diane. "They teach us to take care of ourselves, so we won't be a burden to others."

Diane tossed her head, "Well, you're lucky you found a prince like Jordan who will place your needs above his."

Diane's words sliced like a searing knife into Jessie's heart, but this woman would not get the best of her. "Oh, I'm very lucky. I'm so blessed that I've found my Prince Charming who will sacrifice all for me. Perhaps we do live in a fairy tale world." She cocked her head and flashed a saccharine smile. "I bet you prayed for that."

Diane's jaw dropped from her scarlet face. She lifted her nose in the air and flipped her perfectly styled hair.

"By the way, I hope you sue the mechanic that did this to you," she said as the ladies hustled her out the door.

Vikki wrapped her arms around Jessie's slumped shoulders. "I'm so sorry. I wish you'd never heard those words."

An ache burned in the pit of Jessie's stomach. "It's true, Vikki. What she said is the truth. She's only giving voice to what others think."

"But it's not true, Jessie. Jordan loves you. Your accident doesn't change anything. He doesn't see you as a burden."

"Maybe not now, but what if he does get tired of being a caregiver? And Diane's right, we might not be able to be intimate like— like other people." Tears she'd kept at bay leaked from her lids. "What do I do? How can I move forward?"

Vikki held her hand. "I don't have answers for you, Jessie. But I know one thing. Jordan will always love you. He won't regret marrying you. Have you talked to him about your fears?"

"Yes, but he says we'll figure it all out."

"See, Jordan's a good man."

Jessie managed a smile and brushed a tear from the side of her nose. "But not quite a prince, huh?"

Vikki pursed her lips, "Well, he is charming." At that, both girls dissolved into laughter mingled with tears.

* * *

As Vikki walked toward the hospital's front entrance, she passed a patient care aide hurrying down the hall toting a fluffy looking teddy bear holding a rose in its paw. She smiled. Another bear for Jessie. Hopefully, it would lift her spirits a little. Who could be sending them, though? She continued to the parking lot where Jeremy had left the car earlier and started her drive to Jordan's house. Jeremy would be shocked when she told him about what happened in Jessie's room. And that's not all he would be surprised about if she could find the right moment to talk to him.

That evening over supper, Vikki watched Jeremy's expressions change from amazement to anger and finally to sorrow as she relayed the hospital room incident between Jessie and Diane.

"Are you kidding me? I can't imagine how much pain that caused Jessie."

"Yes, but she did get the last word." Vikki grinned as she repeated Jessie's final remark. "We laughed through our tears picturing Jordan as Prince Charming."

"I'm glad she was able to find a bit of humor," Jeremy said, "But does Jessie really think she's a burden? I know Jordan doesn't see her that way."

"She's doubting. She knows Jordan loves her, but she is afraid he'll get tired of being her caregiver. And Busybody Diane sure didn't help." Vikki felt the warmth rise on her cheeks. She grabbed her plate and stomped to the sink. "And she'd better back off me, too!"

"Hey, what's wrong?" Jeremy walked over to her. "Did Diane say something to you, too?"

"She doesn't think I make a good pastor's wife. And I don't if it means standing beside you each Sunday and being in the limelight making sure I say the right thing at all times."

"Vikki, you know I don't care if you stick by my side every minute. Don't let Diane or anyone else tell you how to act, 'cause I wouldn't want a cookie cutter preacher's wife. I want you." He kissed her nose. "I can talk to Patrick if you want."

Vikki blinked her tears away and twisted her necklace. "No. Don't talk to Patrick. I can handle Diane. Patrick causes you enough grief." She reached up and put her arms around his neck. "I love you, Jeremy."

"And I love you, my beautiful wallflower."

Vikki cleaned up the kitchen while Jeremy read Heather a bedtime story. After her shower, she found her husband sitting in bed reading his nightly devotions.

"Jeremy, after you're done, we need to talk."

"Well, that sounds serious. Sit here beside me while I finish this paragraph. I'm almost done."

Vikki stifled the temptation to pull Jeremy into a hug and tousle his unruly blond hair. Oh, how she loved this man who had stolen her heart the night he shared his struggle dealing with his wife's death. She had thought love would forever elude her after her first husband's betrayal. But God, in his grace, brought them together and broke the chains of anger and guilt that bound Jeremy's soul.

Jeremy swept his bangs to the side. "Shall we pray, or do you want to talk first?"

"Let's go ahead and pray. We might need it. You lead tonight."

"Well, it's sure going to be hard to concentrate, now."

Vikki sat across from Jeremy with her hands in his. Jeremy thanked God for his goodness and prayed for Jessie and Jordan. He finished with a petition for his ability to lead the church.

"Alright," he said after his prayer, "This better be good after all the buildup."

Vikki's heart raced as she met his gaze. "Remember I had an ear infection the week we got married, and I was taking an antibiotic?"

Jeremy gave her a questioning look. "Yes...?"

"And do you know that antibiotics can reduce the effectiveness of birth control pills?"

Jeremy stared at her with parted lips. "Uh, I guess not."

Vikki took a deep breath. "Well, I knew they could, but it slipped my mind until the morning in the lodge as I took my last pill."

Silence reigned for a few seconds, then Jeremy's mouth fell open. "No, you're not…"

"I'm pregnant."

"Oh." Jeremy's eyes were saucers. "I mean that's, that's— wow."

Vikki's hand fluttered to her chest. "Are you upset? I know we talked about waiting a year or two."

"Of course not. I'm surprised but not upset. So it's a little sooner than we planned." One corner of his mouth rose slightly, and his eyes twinkled, "Anyway, it's kinda romantic, you know, a honeymoon baby."

"Yeah. Well, I can just imagine Diane and her crew fervently counting the months to my due date hoping for a scandal."

"So, we'll give them something to talk about. They all just love a juicy story." He lifted her chin. "Don't worry babe, anyone who matters will know the truth about us."

Jeremy fell back on his pillow, and Vikki snuggled next to him. "I think we should wait a little while before we tell anyone, don't you? I mean except for our families maybe."

"I agree. It might be a good diversion for Jessie. She'll be all excited about being an aunt. I'll run it by Jordan at work on Tuesday."

"That's a good idea," Vikki murmured, stroking Jeremy's cheek.

Jeremy propped up his head and looked into her eyes. "This is awesome. Are you happy about it?"

"Yes, a little nervous, but also excited." She felt his lips brush hers in his soft butterfly wings way, leaving her defenseless. "Hey, now, that's not fair."

"Mm-hmm, I know, baby," he said, pulling her close.

CHAPTER SEVEN

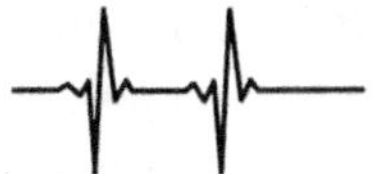

The hospital receptionist greeted Jordan with a warm smile. "Welcome to Hope Rehab. How may I help you?"

"Hi there. I'm hoping you can give me some information that might help me solve a little mystery."

"I can try. What do you need to know?'

"You have a patient named Jessie Marcus, and someone keeps sending her teddy bears with flowers. There's never any name on the tag. Do you know if a flower shop delivers them?"

"Oh, yes, I've taken one to her room. They're not a flower shop delivery. We figured they were from her boyfriend."

"I'm her fiancé, and they aren't from me. What does this guy look like?"

The receptionist straightened her shoulders. "I really haven't paid much attention."

"But you do remember a guy dropping off teddy bears at the desk here."

"We can't give out that kind of information, sir."

Jordan leaned forward and placed his arms on the counter. "Hey, I'm not mad at the guy. Jessie wants to thank whoever he is." The receptionist relaxed a bit. Jordan angled his head and lifted an eyebrow, "Can you at least tell me if he has shoulder-length blond hair? I think he may be a member of our youth group at church."

"That's him. He just sets his gifts on the counter and asks that they be delivered to Jessie's room."

"Yes," Jordan muttered to himself, then grinned at the receptionist, "Thanks for your help, and don't worry, I'm not about to cause any trouble."

Jordan strolled to Jessie's room and peeked in the doorway. Jessie was sitting on the edge of the bed, working on transferring to her wheelchair. Becky, her therapist, stood beside her.

"Use your upper body, Jessie. You can do this," Becky said.

"I can't lift myself."

"Try leaning forward a little."

Jordan winced at Jessie's distressed expression but stayed where he was.

Becky helped her balance on the side of the bed and angled the transfer board a bit more. "Here, try again."

Jessie pushed down with her hands and lifted her hips but sank back on the bed. "I can't do it."

Both ladies lifted their eyes as they heard Jordan's smooth bass voice. "Love lifted me, love lifted me, when nothing else would help, love lifted me."

He walked over and sat on the bed, cradling Jessie in his arms, "Come on guys, sing with me. I learned this when I was a kid." He winked at Becky. "It can't hurt."

He began again, "I was sinking deep in sin far from the peaceful shore, Very deeply stained within, sinking to rise no more, But the master of the sea, Heard my despairing cry, From the waters lifted me, Now safe am I."

Becky and Jessie joined tentatively at first, but their voices filled the room by the end of the chorus. "Love lifted me, love lifted me, when nothing else would do, love lifted me. Love lifted me, love lifted me, When nothing else would do. Love lifted me."

They sang the verse and chorus again as Jessie pushed with her hands, and Jordan gave her a little shove that landed her in her chair. "See, all you need is a little inspiration."

"But you cheated. You helped me."

Jordan opened his eyes wide, "Are you sure it was me?"

Becky laughed, "You are so good for her, Jordan."

"Oh, I don't know," he lifted her chin and tucked a stray curl behind her ear, "I think she's pretty good for me."

Becky gathered her supplies and glanced at her watch. "I think Jessie could use a little break. Why don't you take a stroll before her next session?"

"That sounds good. Want to, Love?"

They headed toward the room with the floor-to-ceiling windows. At one end, French doors led to a courtyard. Two benches with three chairs between them circled a fountain with spaces for wheelchairs on either side. Colorful flowers graced a walking path to another sitting area. Jordan chose a bench, and Jessie wheeled up beside him.

The sweet aroma of lilacs floated in the air. "It's a beautiful day, isn't it?"

"I don't want to be a burden to you, Jordan," Jessie said in a rush of words.

Jordan heard the distress in her voice. How could he make her understand? "Jessie, I love you. I'm willing to care for you."

Jessie's amber eyes flashed. "I don't want your sacrifice, and I don't need you to give up everything for me."

Jordan's breath caught in his throat. "It's not a sacrifice, Jessie. I just meant that I'm here for you."

Jessie bit her lower lip. "I know you believe that. But it would be a sacrifice. You'll have to help me with personal things, like showers and— "

Jordan grinned. "Now, that wouldn't be so bad."

"Stop it, Jordan! Just stop! You can't tease your way around this. Right now, I have a catheter to mess with, and a bowel program. I can't even go to the bathroom on my own. Do you want to deal with those things?"

Jordan felt the heat rise on his neck. "We've been through all that, and I get it. I see you've been talking to your mother again."

"No, I haven't. But at least she understands these issues."

Jordan wanted to scream. Marianne only saw problems. He took a deep breath and tried again. "Jessie, I do understand. I've had some medical training, you know."

"But it's different with me. I'm not just some nameless accident victim you'll never see again. This will be every day, Jordan." She lowered her eyes. "Every day."

Jordan turned her chair around so that she faced him. "I know that, Jessie. I realize there'll be hard times, uncomfortable times, but we can get through them. Can't you trust me?"

Jessie's jaw stiffened, and her words came out in

spurts. "It isn't a matter of trust, Jordan. I know you would marry me tomorrow and be faithful till the end. But I don't want you to give up everything for me. I don't want people pitying you, thinking you are some saint or— or a prince."

Jordan couldn't resist a half-smile picturing himself as a prince. "Where did you get that idea? I don't think there's much danger of me being mistaken for a saint. Maybe a prince, though." He took Jessie's hands. "Who in the world put that thought in your head?"

"I know people will pity you for giving up your life to care for me. And right now, I'm trying to hold myself together. I'm not sure what to do, but I do know I don't want to be a burden to anyone— especially you." She looked up, and her eyes pleaded, "Can't you understand that?"

Regret washed over Jordan as he remembered Jeremy's words from a few nights ago. "I am so sorry, Love. I want to help you through this. I thought," his voice wobbled, "I thought if I tried hard enough, I could take care of everything for you. Jeremy cautioned me against trying to be a hero, but I didn't get it. Please help me understand, Jessie."

A prayer for strength rose in his heart as he stumbled over the words he had to say. "Jessie, you'd never be a burden to me, but you need to make the decision that's best for you. Even if— even if it doesn't include me. I'll be your friend, your husband, whatever you need, for however long it takes." He swiped at the tears threatening to leak from his eyes. "I have to tell you this, though. You're as beautiful and whole to me as you've ever been, and I'm beyond attracted to you. As long as I can hold you close to me, like I said before, we can figure everything else out."

Jessie's eyes filled, and a tear traced her cheek, "Thank you, Jordan. I know God sent you to me. You drew me back to faith by looking beyond my past and assuring me of God's love despite all my rebellion and bad decisions."

Jordan longed to take her in his arms and kiss her in a way that would make her believe he was more than a guide leading her back to faith, but instead, he rose to his feet and said with a mischievous smile, "We need to get you back before they think I've whisked you off to my palace."

* * *

Jordan shielded his eyes from the late afternoon sun as he drove toward the mechanic's shop. Now that he had confirmed that Aiden was sending the bears, he needed to know why. A jingle announced his arrival, and Amber met him with a cool stare.

"What can I do for you?"

"I need to speak with a teen you have working for you named Aiden."

"Listen, Mister uh,"

"Jordan."

"Listen, Jordan. I've told you all I know about the Mustang we worked on for your fiancée." She crossed her arms, "And I'm sorry about her accident, but I don't have any other information to give you."

"That's fine because I didn't come to talk with you. I need to see Aiden."

Amber glanced away, then looked up at Jordan. "Aiden called in sick today. And he probably won't be back all week."

"Hmm. I don't suppose you'll tell me where he lives."

"I can't tell you that."

"But you can tell me if he worked on the Mustang."

Amber shuffled some papers on the counter. "My service manager, Randy, oversees the work the mechanics complete. We have safety procedures in place when we change tires. I can assure you that the tires were put on correctly."

"But Jessie's wheel did fall off after she picked up the car from this shop."

Amber glared at him. "Wheels can fall off for several reasons. The wheel stud could break or even the axle. I stand by my employees. You need to leave now, or I'll call the police. I won't answer any more questions without a lawyer."

Jordan stepped back; glad no other customers were around the service desk. "Amber, there's no need to call anyone. I didn't come here to make accusations."

A wiry man approached the front desk. A glance at the title on his shirt told Jordan he was the service manager.

"Need any help, Amber?" he peered at Jordan. "This guy bothering you?"

"No, Randy, it's ok. He wanted to talk with Aiden, but I told him Aiden was out sick."

Jordan noticed the lines on Randy's forehead scrunch up a bit as he shifted his eyes toward Amber. "Oh, uh, that's right. So what's this guy's problem?"

"Nothing, sir," Jordan said. "I'm just leaving. Have a great day."

Jordan looked in the shop window as he turned his key in the ignition. Randy was still at the counter, engaged in discussion with Amber. Something didn't feel right. He hadn't considered looking for Aiden's car earlier, but now he scanned the lot. No blue sedan sat in front of the shop. He drove around to the back of the building and looked through the open garage doors. A mechanic was working on a car raised on a lift, but there was no sign of Aiden.

Then he saw it. A blue Malibu with rust along the top of the wheel wells sat in the far corner of the lot. He was sure it was the car he'd seen Aiden get into at the hospital. As Jordan hopped out of his truck, Aiden rounded the corner of the building and headed toward his car. Jordan froze, and Aiden turned to him with a shocked look.

"Leave me alone!" Aiden shouted and ran to his car.

Jordan uttered a rare curse as he watched Aiden tear out of the lot. He couldn't follow him after his conversation with Amber unless he wanted cops to show up on his doorstep. He climbed back in his truck and pulled around to the front of the shop to see Amber and Randy staring at him. He blew out a puff of air, "Great."

* * *

Aiden kept his eye on the rearview mirror. Jordan's truck was nowhere in sight. Thankfully, Amber had been able to stall him for a few minutes. She must have believed his story about Jordan stalking him. But after Jordan's visit, she might figure out that his mistake caused the tire to fall off of the Mustang. And now, since Jordan had seen him bolt out the back door, he'd be suspicious.

Aiden drove aimlessly for a few miles, then pulled into a grocery store lot and killed the engine. What a mess he'd made of things. Jordan had seen him at church, the hospital, and now the shop. Jordan would put the pieces together and know he was the guilty one, the one responsible for Jessie being in a wheelchair.

Aiden always discussed his problems with his father, but he couldn't burden his dad with this one. With his MS attacks occurring more often, his dad had enough to handle. One thing his father taught him was the value of integrity. A confession to Jessie was mandatory, but he couldn't fathom how to do it. Right now, though, he needed to get groceries, medical supplies for his dad, and a teddy bear.

CHAPTER EIGHT

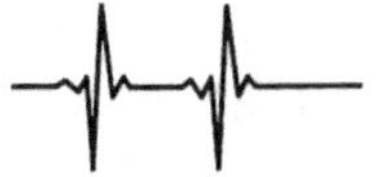

On Tuesday morning, Jordan ambled into the fire station and found Jeremy sorting through medical supplies. "Hey Preacher Boy, what are you doing here so early? Tryin' to make me look bad?"

"Hi, Jordan," Jeremy said with a smile, "There's still plenty to do. I was a little restless this morning, so I came in early."

"Something on your mind?"

"Just Jessie, and… you know."

Jordan understood. The two men marked off daily safety checklists and then gathered and inspected the medical supplies. After ensuring the readiness of each emergency vehicle, they organized their equipment and gear so they would be ready to take immediate action. Other employees filed in and began their daily preparations.

After the two men finished the last of their duties, they walked to a small table in the lounge area to have coffee and relax before beginning their day.

"I do have something to tell you," Jeremy said, setting his mug down.

Jordan looked over the newspaper he was reading. "What's up?"

"Well, um, I guess I'm going to be a father."

Jordan let his paper fall to the table and stared at Jeremy. "You guess? What do you mean? You're already a father!"

"I know that. I mean I'm going to be a father again," Jeremy pushed his bangs off his forehead, "Vikki's pregnant."

"Well, you sure didn't waste any time. When's this gonna happen?"

Jeremy shifted in his seat. "In a little more than seven months, I guess. I didn't ask her the due date, but, you know, it couldn't be more than that."

Jordan eyed his friend with amusement. "You guess you're going to be a father again. You guess it'll be in seven months. You want to guess how this happened?"

"Oh, stop it. I thought you'd be happy for me."

"I am happy for you. Are you okay with it?" Jordan said with a teasing smile.

"Of course I'm okay with it. It's a little sooner than we planned, but we're very excited."

"Aw, Preacher Boy," Jordan said with sparkling eyes, "You should've come to me. I could have explained how to avoid this."

"Ah. Is that right?"

"Hey, at least I listened in health class."

Jeremy shook his head and laughed. "Vikki was on medication that interfered—"

Jordan held up his hand. "Nix it, Preacher. You've got nothing to explain. It's all cool. Jessie will be thrilled to hear it, that is, when you're actually sure," he said with a wink.

"We thought she would be. We want to keep it quiet for now, but we'll let Jessie know."

Jordan's bantering was interrupted as a policeman approached the table. "Hey, Officer Trent. What brings you around here?"

"I need to talk to you, actually."

Jordan raised his brows, "What about?"

The policeman glanced at Jeremy. "Do you want to go somewhere more private?"

"No, Preacher's fine."

Officer Trent shrugged. "Okay, then. What's going on between you and a young man named Aiden?"

Jordan crossed his arms. "Nothing, I just want to talk to him."

"Well, it seems he doesn't feel the same way. Someone's asked for a restraining order against you."

"A restraining order? All I want to do is talk to the guy. I haven't threatened him or anything."

Jeremy looked at the officer. "That's right, Trent. Jordan wants to find out some information about work done on Jessie's car before the accident."

"I get that, but apparently, Aiden doesn't want to talk." Officer Trent grabbed a chair and straddled it.

"Listen, Jordan. I know you're no threat to this guy, and I couldn't serve a restraining order on you if I wanted to."

Jordan frowned. "Why's that?'

"Because Aiden didn't request it," Trent said, raising his palms.

"What?" Jordan exchanged looks with Jeremy. "What's that supposed to mean?"

"It means someone else requested that you stay away

from Aiden. A judge wouldn't issue an order in that case."

Amber's face popped into Jordan's mind. "Then why are you here? And who requested it?"

"To try to keep you out of trouble. I promised the complainant that I would warn you to keep away from Aiden, so an order wouldn't be necessary." He rubbed the side of his nose. "You know I can't give you a name."

"I can guess who it is anyway." Jordan felt his fists ball up as they dropped on the table. "I need answers, Trent. I want to know if someone in that shop made a careless mistake that caused Jessie's tire to fall off her car."

"Is she planning to sue?"

"Not that I know of. I thought the company's insurance company might be able to help with medical bills, though. I'm not out for revenge. I just need to know. If I could talk to Aiden, that's all I want. I think he's hiding something he knows about what happened to Jessie's car. And she's protecting him."

"She?"

"Yeah, I'm sure Amber, the shop's manager, is behind this. She lied about Aiden being sick the day I went to talk to him, and she threatened to call the police if I didn't leave."

"And did you leave?"

"Of course. You know me, Trent."

Trent tilted his head. "Yeah, I know you. I know you won't let this go," the officer said as he rose. "Be careful, Jordan, and quit following the kid around. Hire a lawyer for legal advice before you do anything else." He shot Jeremy a sideways glance, "Keep a leash on him, okay?"

Jeremy angled his head. "I'll try, officer, but that's a tall order."

* * *

Aiden maneuvered his Malibu through traffic, squinting into the sun streaming through his windshield. He needed to get to Hope Rehabilitation Hospital before Jessie had any visitors. Would he be brave enough to carry out his plan? He had debated it all night, but he knew what he had to do in the end. Though a confession note taped to the bear and left at the counter would be much easier, his sense of honor won out. He would be a man of integrity.

How would Jessie react when he told her? Aiden shuddered at the thought. Would she scream at him? Throw things? Tell him how he had ruined her life?

Aiden's stomach churned, and he turned abruptly into a drugstore parking lot. He cracked the window to the cool morning air, clutched his rolling gut, and rocked back and forth. Maybe he should turn around and go to the shop, confess to Amber, and let her decide what to do. But no, Amber might get sued, and it wasn't her fault. He couldn't do that to her, not after she had given him a chance. He wasn't a child anymore.

He waited for his queasiness to ease, then pulled back into the traffic to complete his journey. He parked near the back of the lot and forced his trembling fingers to unfasten his seatbelt. Drops of sweat beaded on his forehead and slid down his cheeks. He swiped the side of his face, breathed a wordless prayer to a God he wasn't sure existed, and grabbed the stuffed bear from the seat beside him. Somehow, he forced one foot in front of the other until he reached the revolving door. He stepped inside and considered following the door until he landed outside again, but instead buried his face in the bear's fur and stepped into the hospital.

* * *

An image Jessie scarcely recognized peered at her from the mirror as she plunged her toothbrush into its holder. Whose hollow face gazed back at her? Where were the eyes that shone with joyful anticipation of planning a wedding? Where was the confident woman who worked as a buyer for a clothing business? She squeezed her eyes shut. Maybe it was all a dream. She would awaken, rise from this cursed chair, and run out the door into freedom, back to the world she knew before being cruelly snatched away.

Nurses and therapists praised her determination and assured her she could navigate the reality that was now her life. But their words were meaningless. She didn't ask for this. Echoes of her former existence swirled behind her eyelids: images of a girl in a red Mustang with her hair blowing in the wind, Jordan's brown eyes melting into hers on a moonlit night as he kissed her.

She opened her eyes, and they fell to the useless limbs that now trapped her, to the sight of the bag filled with pale yellow fluid strapped on her leg. The hollowed-eyed image in the mirror belonged to her. She hurled her paper cup at the mirror and watched the water splatter against the glass rolling down like tears.

A tap on her door halted her thoughts. "Jessie?"

"Come in, Vikki. I'm in the bathroom getting ready for the day."

Vikki leaned against the door frame. "Are you okay?"

"I've been better. I'm glad you came to visit. I could use a friend to talk to."

"I'm here to listen."

"I know. I'll be lonely when you go back to work."

"Having summers off is a good thing about teaching."

Vikki patted Jessie's shoulder. "I'll still come to see you and so will other people. Besides, you'll probably be out of here by then."

"Hopefully. But where I'll go or what I'll do, I have no idea."

"Jessie, whatever decision you make, your friends and family will support you."

Jessie forced a smile and wheeled into the room. "Look at the flowers the church sent.

The benefit for me is next Saturday night. My therapist, Becky, said the doctor would let me attend. It will be my first night out in the real world."

"That's great! You'll go, won't you?"

Jessie felt the warmth creep up her face, "I want to, but, well, I haven't decided— you know about Jordan and me."

"It's okay, Jessie. Jordan's made it clear that whatever money is raised will go to help with your medical costs even if you don't get married right away."

A knock on the door and the sight of a young man clutching a teddy bear to his chest interrupted their conversation.

Jessie's jaw dropped as she stared at her mystery gift giver. "You're the one." She narrowed her eyes, "Do I know you?"

The young man cleared his throat, "I, uh, came to the youth group a couple of times. "I'm Aiden."

"Oh, yes, I remember seeing you, but why…" she bit her lower lip, "Why have you been sending me teddy bears?"

Aiden shuffled his feet. "Because Jordan teased you about liking them one night."

"Oh." Jessie looked at him in confusion, "But why are you sending them to me now?"

Aiden squeezed the stuffed bear tighter as tears welled in his eyes.

"Aiden, what's wrong?" Vikki said, taking a step closer to him.

A chill swept through Jessie's body as she remembered the message on every card attached to the teddy bears —I'm sorry. "What are you trying to tell me?" she breathed.

Aiden's face blanched a ghostly hue. "Your wreck was my fault! It's my fault." He stumbled to the wall and trembled against it.

"Oh, Aiden," Vikki said.

Jessie fixed incredulous eyes on the sobbing teen. Words she couldn't bring to voice pushed against the edge of her lips until they burst out in a husky moan. "How? Why?" She rolled closer to Aiden.

Vikki placed her hand on the arm of Jessie's chair and spoke to the teen in a hushed tone. "Tell us what happened, Aiden. It's okay."

"I got called away while working on your car. I— I didn't finish tightening all the lug nuts." Aiden sucked in several breaths and squeezed his eyes shut pushing out more tears. "I'm so sorry."

Vikki eyed him. "You mean you forgot about it?"

"I didn't expect the car to be gone when I got back, so I thought Randy must have finished the job. Aiden shook his head, "But I guess he didn't. It wasn't his responsibility. It was mine," he choked out in a barely audible voice.

Jessie gaped at him. "I — I don't know what to say to you." Hot tears rolled from her eyes and dripped onto her lips.

Aiden shoved the bear into her lap. "I'm so sorry. It's all my fault."

Jessie buried her face in the bear's soft fur. "It was an accident. You," she breathed short whiffs of air up her nose, "didn't mean it."

Vikki touched his shoulder. "Aiden, you didn't set out to hurt anyone."

Aiden's face crumpled, and he nodded toward Jessie. "But I did hurt her." He swiped at his eyes and ran out of the room.

Jessie stared at the door for several seconds. Somewhere in the back of her mind, she had convinced herself the accident was a freak of nature beyond human error. She hadn't dared believe otherwise. Having no one to blame made it easier to accept somehow. But now, a young man's confession destroyed her wall of protection. She was at a loss on how to deal with it.

Vikki sat on the edge of the bed, her eyes radiating the shock of Aiden's confession. She held onto the cross dangling from her necklace. "Jessie, are you okay?"

"I don't know." She closed her eyes and breathed deeply, trying to collect her scattered emotions. "What do I do now?"

Vikki rested her chin on her fingertips. "I don't know. Why don't I help you get dressed, and we can get you something from the cafe? You don't look well."

Jessie leaned forward and covered her face with her hands. "I think I need orange juice or a soda."

Vikki reached for the call button, but Jessie touched her wrist. "No, don't. Hand me that can. There's a little left in it." She took a few sips and handed it to Vikki. "I need to get out of this room. Let's get something to eat and sit in the courtyard for a bit."

* * *

Aiden wrapped his fingers around the steering wheel. He stared out the window as the scene he'd been a part of replayed in his mind. He pictured himself walking down the hall clutching the teddy bear. He saw himself forcing his hand to knock on the door. The following events were muddled, but Jessie's tragic look of shock would be etched in his mind forever. It was over. He'd faced Jessie and confessed his guilt, but would he ever be able to forgive himself? Putting the car in gear, he drove out of the lot, eyeing his rearview mirror until the hospital faded from sight.

* * *

Jeremy hopped out of the ambulance after returning from a brush fire that had gotten out of hand. Luckily, the firefighters were able to quench the flames quickly. The owner was treated for smoke inhalation and then taken to the hospital for observation.

After helping care for the vehicles and showering, Jeremy sat down to a late afternoon lunch. Jordan pulled out a chair across from him.

"Well, our quiet morning disappeared quickly," Jeremy said between bites of his sandwich.

"Yeah, sometimes those minor runs can take a toll on you, especially three before noon." Jordan took a swig of his soda. "But hey, that's what we do. At least it cured your restlessness."

Jeremy's phone chimed. "Hmm, it's a text from Vikki. She wants me to call."

Jordan gave him a mischievous smile. "Go ahead and call her. I'll leave you two lovebirds alone. Maybe she wants to clear up this fatherhood thing for you." He pushed his chair back and stood. "I have a book to read anyway."

"Really, you read books?" Jeremy tossed after him.

Jordan raised his thumb in the air. "Good one, Preacher Boy."

Jeremy tapped Vikki's name and waited. She rarely asked him to call her from the station. "Hi, baby, what's up?" His eyes grew round as he listened. "You're kidding me! It was Aiden? Jordan thought he knew something."

Jeremy listened for several minutes. "I'm glad you spent time with Jessie this afternoon. I'll let Jordan know what happened. We won't be out of here until tomorrow morning."

Jeremy disconnected and set off to locate Jordan. He found him in the kitchen wiping the counter. "Hey, I need to talk to you."

"What now? Does Vikki need me to explain things to you?" Jordan looked up, and his smile faded. "What's wrong?"

Jeremy relayed the information about Aiden's confession and Jessie's reaction. "Vikki said Jessie felt better after she had time to process everything and was concerned for Aiden's well-being."

"I knew it! I knew Aiden was involved in some way because of those teddy bears. I wish I'd been able to talk to him. Now he's afraid of me. It was a careless accident, but it doesn't seem entirely his fault."

"You're right. Part of the responsibility falls on the service manager. He should have checked his work since Aiden was called away."

Jordan smacked the countertop. "Then Amber was protecting Aiden along with her own hide. You bet I'll be paying her a visit tomorrow."

"What? Didn't you listen to Trent? He told you to lay off and have Jessie hire a lawyer."

"Officer Trent told me to stay away from Aiden, not Amber. I'm going to talk to her. She either lied to me or at least suspected it was Aiden, and I'm going to find out what's going on."

"But what will that get you? You can't afford to jeopardize your job."

"Good grief, Jeremy, simmer down. I'm not going to cause a scene. And the only money I'm interested in would be for Jessie's medical costs. I'm sure the shop has insurance for that. Besides," he met Jeremy's eyes, "Aren't you a little worried about Aiden since Vikki told you how upset he was?"

Jeremy sighed. He knew Jordan had a point about Aiden, but he wasn't sure about Jordan's motives. He ran his fingers through his bangs. "I'll go with you then."

Jordan flashed a sassy smile. "Well, you do have to keep a leash on me."

Jeremy snatched the towel, "I'll finish up here. You need to call Jessie."

* * *

Vikki stayed until late afternoon, comforting Jessie as she came to terms with Aiden's confession. After she left, Jordan called to check on her but didn't press for details. He promised to visit the following afternoon. Now, Jessie lay in her bed waiting for sleep. She stared at the dimly lit door that had ushered in the soul-wrenching news that added another layer of hurt to her tormented heart.

A tear leaked from her lower eyelid. "God. Where are you?" She squeezed her fingernails into the palm of her hands. "I hate this. I hate being trapped in a wheelchair." Heaviness pushed on her chest. "Do you care? Is this all there is for me?"

Tears of anguish and despair flooded her lower lids, soaking her pillow. She reached into the darkness with outstretched hands. "Please, God. I need you." A breath of warm air drifted over her, and she fell into the most peaceful sleep she'd had since the accident.

CHAPTER NINE

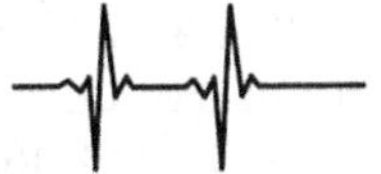

Aiden sank between the twisted roots of a crooked tree whose branches dangled over the murmuring creek. He leaned against the trunk and tilted the forbidden flask shuddering as the burn of the golden liquid slipped past his tongue. He blew out a long breath. Why did people drink this stuff? His father took a shot occasionally when the pain of his spasms became intense, but he'd stressed the dangers of alcohol abuse over and over. Aiden imagined the disappointment in his father's eyes if he'd known Aiden's plans.

Earlier that evening, Aiden had grabbed the bottle and hid it under his sweatshirt jacket before tossing his dad a quick excuse about going to the store. Movie characters drown their sorrows in alcohol, so he would try it, even though the few times he'd experimented with alcohol, it had left him feeling lousy.

After his mother's death at the hands of a drunk driver, he and his father muddled through. And until his father's illness, they lived comfortably on his mechanic's salary. The tight budget they lived on now was one of the reasons Aiden dropped out of school to work full-time.

Aiden promised his father he would finish school online. He knew his father didn't like his new friends, so it made it easier for him to agree to Aiden's plan to quit going to school. Aiden had always been a loner, but these guys invited him to play video games, drink beer, and hang out. The night Aiden stumbled home with bloodshot eyes and a musky, slightly foul smell on his clothes, his father put an end to his association with those friends. Aiden didn't balk much; he knew that road would lead to trouble.

Aiden raised the bottle to his lips. Maybe he would drink until he passed out. If he didn't wake up, what would it matter? Jessie might be happy if he were dead, and he wouldn't have to face the look in his father's eyes when he heard about his horrible mistake. But that would be the coward's way out. He imagined his father alone in his chair, mourning his son's death and took another gulp.

He lowered his head on his palms. Giving Jessie teddy bears had been a stupid idea. What made him think a stuffed bear could erase his mistake? How could he live knowing he'd ruined someone's life?

A breeze danced over the creek forming shimmering waves under the clear starlit sky. Aiden gazed into the night. "God, are you up there? Is my mom with you like Dad told me?" He took a final swig of the fiery liquid and poured the rest on the ground, watching it carve snake-like rivers as it trickled along the bank. He yawned, rose halfway to his feet, wobbled and slid back against the tree. That last swig had worked a number on him. He closed his eyes and leaned his head on the rough bark.

"Aiden, is that you?"

Aiden shielded his eyes against the early morning sun and jumped to his feet. "Who is it?"

"It's okay. It's me, Vikki." Her eyes fell on the empty bottle. "What are you doing here?"

"What do you want? Did Jessie send you to find me?"

"No, Jeremy had an errand to run after his shift at the fire station, so I decided to take a walk while I waited. We're meeting at the church later." Vikki's green eyes grew round. "I wasn't looking for you. Are you hiding?"

"Oh yeah, the park borders the church property," he muttered. "No, I'm not hiding. I came here to think, and I guess I fell asleep."

"Hmm…, Jack Daniels. Did you drink all this?"

Aiden grabbed the bottle. "No! I poured most of it in the creek."

"Well, I guess the fish are feeling no pain."

Aiden grunted. "Or they have a huge headache," he said, rubbing his temples.

"Would you let me take you to get something to eat? It might help you feel better."

Aiden hesitated, but kindness shone from Vikki's eyes. His stomach rumbled. "I guess so. I don't want to go home yet."

"Alright, let's find a restaurant. I've got time. Jeremy has work to do at the church this morning, so he won't mind if I'm late."

* * *

With a reluctant looking tag-along trailing him, Jordan pushed through the door to Claymon's Mechanic Shop. "Hello, Amber."

Amber squared her shoulders and beckoned her service manager to the counter. "Randy, will you finish up with this customer?"

She led them out of the customer's earshot, "What do you want? I told you I have no more information for you."

Jordan took a deep breath. "I need to talk to Aiden. It's important."

"He's not here."

"Where is he, then?"

"I don't know."

"Come on, Amber. You lied to me the last time I was here. What are you protecting him from? And why the restraining order?"

"A restraining order? I don't know what you're talking about."

Jordan bit his upper lip and glanced at Jeremy.

"Listen, Amber, we aren't here to cause trouble." Jeremy stepped closer and lowered his voice. "We know about Aiden's mistake." His eyes swept the room. "Is there anywhere we could talk privately?"

Amber sighed. "We can sit in the office. Let me get Randy to watch the counter."

Jordan grinned as she walked away. "Good job, Preacher Boy. You're amazing."

"It's in my blood, you know."

Amber returned, and the two men followed her to the office. She sat at the desk and motioned to the chairs in front of it. "Tell me what this is all about."

Jordan scanned her face. "Officer Trent told us

someone asked for a restraining order to keep me away from Aiden. I assumed it was you."

Amber shook her head. "No, it wasn't me. I did lie about Aiden not being here that day because he said you were following him. But I didn't ask for a restraining order. I didn't even call the police."

Jordan scrunched his eyebrows. "I don't understand." Was she protecting Aiden? "Do you know that Aiden forgot to tighten the lug nuts on Jessie's wheel?"

"What? Who told you that?"

"Aiden told Jessie," Jeremy said. "He went to the hospital and confessed everything."

"But, but that's not true! Randy finished the Mustang." Amber stood up. "He needs to hear this. I'll get someone to watch the counter."

"What's going on? Randy said as he dragged a folding chair through the door. "Did he bring a lawyer this time?"

"No, Randy. This is Jeremy. He's Jessie's brother."

Randy dropped into the chair. "Oh."

Amber nodded to Randy. "Apparently, Aiden went to see Jessie and told her that he was to blame for her car's wheel falling off. But that's not what you told me, and Aiden never said anything like that. Are you covering for him?"

A look of confusion crossed Randy's face. "I'm not covering for Aiden. I told you I finished the job. I tightened the lug nuts on the wheel he was working on and checked all the others like I always do."

Jordan frowned. "Then why would the tire fall off?"

"That's what bugs me." Randy's expression tightened. "I looked at that car a dozen times after the wreck. All the studs were broken off, but the tie rod was in one piece. So was the ball joint. Everything points to loose lug nuts, but I'm telling you I tightened them."

Jordan leaned forward. "If that's true, then how do you explain what happened?"

"I can't. Unless somebody messed with them."

"Are you trying to say someone loosened them?"

Randy shrugged. "Does Jessie have any enemies?"

"That's crazy. The car was here the whole time. Unless Aiden," Jordan looked from Randy to Amber, "Unless Aiden loosened them and made up a story for Jessie."

Amber jumped to her feet. "Aiden would never do that. He's a good kid. Why would you say that?"

"I don't know. People do crazy things."

"No. Aiden had nothing to do with it. I'm sure of it."

Jeremy walked to the window. "Was the Mustang in the shop all night?"

"No," Randy said. "I parked it in the lot so Jessie could pick it up."

Uneasiness stirred the contents in Jordan's stomach. "Do you have security cameras in your lot?"

Amber joined Jeremy at the window. "Yes, but who would come to a car lot and loosen the lug nuts off one car? That doesn't make sense."

"It doesn't make sense unless someone knew Jessie's car was here," Jeremy said. "Maybe someone holds a grudge against her."

"Wait. You're suggesting someone waited for Jessie's car to be parked in the lot so he could loosen her wheel? That kind of stuff only happens in movies."

Jordan shot Jeremy a look. "Maybe Aiden loosened them and is trying to pass it off as a mistake."

Randy's eyes narrowed. "No way! Like Amber said, Aiden may think he's to blame, but I'm telling you that I tightened those wheels. I know I did." He pushed his chair away and stood facing Jordan.

Jordan rose also. "I'm talking about someone loosening those lug nuts while the car sat in the lot."

Randy's mouth twisted, and he took a step closer to Jordan. "You're saying someone loosened them on purpose?"

Jeremy stepped between the two men. "Calm down, Randy. Would we be able to look back at the video data?"

Randy backed away, still glaring at Jordan. "We'd have to ask the owner of the shop."

"Any reason not to?"

Randy sighed. "I don't want to take him on some wild goose chase."

"Randy's right," Amber agreed. "Ben bought the place from Mr. Jenkins when he retired. We'd have to get his permission to check out the videos. I already know one camera isn't working. I called the tech a month ago to come out and fix it."

Jordan's fist punched the palm of his hand. "Let's at least take a look at the camera that's not working. Maybe someone disabled it."

"Alright, we'll take a look. I'll have to get a ladder."

The camera was positioned to have a broad view of the lot and would pick up any motion near the area mechanics parked customers' cars. Amber climbed the ladder but couldn't quite reach the camera.

Jordan peered up at where the lens should be and shook his head. "I can't see anything. Let me climb up."

Jordan climbed the ladder, his eyes searching for the lens. He reached the camera and caught his breath as his fingers ran across an uneven surface. "Hey, somebody's painted the lens black. That's why it won't pick up anything."

Three pairs of eyes stared at Jordan as he approached the ground. Amber spoke first. "You've got to be kidding. Who would do that?"

"Someone who might want to tamper with a vehicle."

"We need to view the security video," Jeremy said. "That way we could figure out the date this camera quit recording."

Amber's jaw dropped. "You think someone painted the lens so they could sabotage Jessie's car?"

Jordan started for the door. "Let's go see if we can find out."

Randy grabbed Jordan's arm. "Hold on, mister. You can't just barge in and look at camera footage. Amber told you we have to ask Ben."

Jordan took a deep calming breath. "Okay, Randy, is Ben here?"

"No. He doesn't come around every day."

Jeremy laid his hand on Jordan's shoulder. "Why don't we give them time to talk with Ben?" He turned to Amber. "Would that work? Will you discuss this with him and get back with us?"

"Ben will probably want to look at the video first. I'll call you, okay?"

Frustration colored Jordan's voice. "Doesn't seem like we have much choice."

Jordan hoisted himself into his truck after they left the shop. A distinguished looking gray-haired man carrying a briefcase crossed in front of the vehicle and walked to the shop door. Jordan tilted his head. There was something familiar in the guy's profile.

Jeremy pointed out the window. "I bet that's Ben."

The man glanced at the truck as he opened the shop door. "He looks like someone I've seen before."

"Yeah, I get the same feeling. Let's get out of here."

* * *

Aiden looked up from his half-eaten sausage burrito when Vikki spoke.

"It took a lot of courage for you to talk to Jessie."

His mouth opened, but he looked away. "So."

"So, most adults wouldn't do that. It shows your integrity."

"Yeah, I've got integrity. Jessie's in a wheelchair. Fair trade, huh?"

Vikki blinked. "That's not what I meant. It was an accident, Aiden. Jessie knows that."

He stared at her for a long minute. "Can we go now? And uh, thank you for breakfast."

Aiden relaxed as the music from Vikki's radio eased the silence on the drive back to the park. Vikki pulled alongside the blue Malibu, "Where are you going now?"

"I don't know. I really don't." He opened his door.

"Wait, Aiden. You need to come clean with your boss. She'll find out anyway." She touched his arm. "Wouldn't it be better if it came from you?"

Aiden's throat burned with bile. "I can't. Amber will fire me. Maybe call the cops."

"It was a mistake, Aiden. If you go now, she'll know you aren't trying to hide anything. I'll go with you."

Something in her eyes made him trust her. "What do you think she'll say?"

"I don't know, but it wasn't all your fault. Amber knew you left before you were finished. Someone should have checked the car. I think it's something you have to do."

"Why?"

"Because of who you want to be."

Aiden gazed at her, unsure why she seemed to care about him. "Okay, I will if you come with me."

As they neared the store, Aiden recognized the blue truck pulling out of the lot and felt his legs weaken. "That's Jordan. He's already told her."

Vikki parked. "Maybe, but if he did you've got nothing to lose. Come on." She pointed toward the road as Jordan spun the pickup and returned to the lot. "Look."

Aiden slammed the door as Jordan's truck drew beside them. "I knew I shouldn't have let you talk me into this."

"Aiden," Jordan called. "Wait up!"

Aiden forced himself not to run and lifted his jaw. "What do you want?"

"The truth. Come inside with me. You need to hear something."

Aiden started for the car, but Vikki took his arm and guided him through the door. Randy and Amber met them with surprised looks.

Jordan said, "Randy, tell Aiden what you told me a few minutes ago. Tell him about the lug nuts."

Randy looked directly at Aiden. "I tightened the lug nuts when you got called away, Aiden. You didn't cause the wheel to come off."

Aiden brought his hand to his mouth. "What?" His knees buckled beneath him.

Jeremy slid a chair up to him. "Here, sit down."

"It wasn't your fault, Aiden. I know I tightened the lug nuts. Then I parked the car in the lot."

"But how did the wheel come off, then?"

"That's what we're trying to find out," Jordan said. "Do you know there are security cameras in the parking lot?"

"Yes, why?"

Jordan ignored the withering look Jeremy shot him. "There's a camera that's not working, Aiden. Someone painted the lens black."

Aiden closed his eyes and tried to sort out the words that muddled his mind. "Why would someone do that?" His mouth gaped as he looked at Jordan. "You don't think I did it, do you?"

Jordan's expression softened. "No, Aiden. I have to say it crossed my mind, but not anymore."

Aiden's temples throbbed. "But you think someone loosened the lug nuts on purpose?"

"Yes, and we need to figure out who. But right now, we need to pay Jessie a visit. And by the way, I never hated you even when I thought you made a mistake with the lug nuts."

Aiden let go of the tension he'd kept in check, and it flowed from him in tears of relief. He gripped the sides of his chair. "What will she say?"

"We won't know until we tell her." Jordan pulled Aiden to his feet and wrapped his arm around his shoulder. "Come on, buddy. I'll take you there now."

CHAPTER TEN

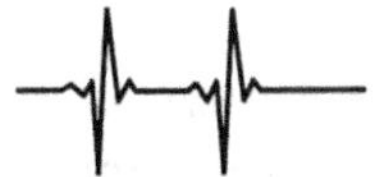

Jessie smiled and waved as Vikki approached the courtyard. "I'm over here." She patted the cool stone of the bench beside her.

"Hi. Are you okay?"

"I am now. Yesterday, when Aiden told me the wreck wasn't his fault after all, we were both a mess. It's awful he had to go through the agony of confessing something that wasn't his fault."

"But he's alright now?"

Jessie hugged her arms. "Aiden and I cried like babies. Poor Jordan didn't know what to do. When our tears dried up, he cracked some silly joke about putting on wading boots. Aiden and I laughed so much that a nurse came to check on us."

"Oh, Jessie, Jordan's such a good guy."

Jessie bit her lower lip and blinked.

"I'm sorry. I didn't mean to push."

"It's okay. I'll figure it out." She smiled at herself using Jordan's phrase.

"I've been waiting to tell you something." Color rose

in Vikki's cheeks, and she held the cross of her necklace. "I'm going to have a baby."

"That's marvelous! When are you due?"

"In about seven months."

"Awesome. I'm going to be an aunt. Does Jordan know?"

"Yes, Jeremy told him, but I wanted to tell you myself."

"I'm so happy for you guys."

They visited until the time for Jessie's therapy session neared. "I'll walk with you to your room," Vikki said. "Remember the benefit is this Saturday. You are going, aren't you?"

"Yes, Jordan picked up an extra shift to get the weekend off, so he's expecting me. I'm excited to get out, but also a little worried."

Vikki stopped at Jessie's door. "You'll be fine. Don't put pressure on yourself. Promise?"

"Promise. I'm off to therapy now. See you Saturday."

* * *

The low-hanging sun shot rays of golden light dancing between the courtyard garden flowers. Jessie breathed in the sweet air bathed with fragrance. She savored the moment wishing it would linger, but the sun continued its skyward journey, shortening the shadows it cast. Jessie ran nervous fingers through her curls and exited the courtyard as Saturday demanded its rightful progression.

"Are you ready for the concert?" Becky called from the doorway of Jessie's room early that evening.

"As ready as I'll ever be."

"You'll have fun, and we can leave whenever you want."

They pulled into the church parking lot, and Jessie frowned as Becky guided the van into a handicapped space. "It seems strange to park here. Something else to get used to, I guess."

Becky lowered the ramp, and Jordan jogged up to the van. "Hi, Love."

The warm evening air greeted Jessie as she glided down the ramp. "This is a perfect night."

Jordan gazed at her. "You bet it is."

The stage sat at the edge of the church property bordering the community park. People carrying foldable camp chairs and blankets scattered themselves in loosely formed rows facing the platform.

Kids from the youth group ran up to Jessie. Jordan stood beside her as she greeted them. Her awestruck eyes scanned the scene. It looked like the entire congregation had shown up to support her. Jordan guided her to a place near the rear of the crowd where Vikki and Jeremy waited.

"I thought you might feel more comfortable back here, but we can move closer if you want," Jordan said.

"No, this is fine. Thanks." She gestured to her therapist. "You all know Becky."

They settled in to enjoy the night. Robbie's band played a mix of contemporary Christian and classic rock, and his clear tenor floated over the crowd. "They sound better every time I hear them," Jessie said. The crowd sang along, and people near the front of the stage danced to the beat.

Jeremy pointed to a couple a few feet away. "I'm not sure Patrick agrees. Look at the scowl on his face. Rock music played on church property is a sin in his book."

Jordan laughed. "You got that right. He nearly wigged out watching your hot dance moves at the wedding reception." He stood and swiveled his hips. "Zzzzz-ouch!"

Jeremy waved him off. "Funny." He looked in the couple's direction. "Well, look who's coming."

"Why, Jessie, how nice to see you here," Diane said as she strutted up to the group. "I wasn't sure you'd be able to come. But luckily, you have Jordan to help you. Oh, and of course your nurse."

Jessie pasted a smile on her face. "Of course. I wouldn't miss it."

Diane patted Jordan's hand. "You're such a prince. Jessie won't even need her nurse with you around."

Jordan's jaw dropped.

Please don't say anything, Jessie prayed silently. Desperate to change the subject, she blurted, "Hey, did you know Vikki's pregnant?" She flinched at Vikki's expression, which now mirrored Jordan's look of shock.

"I know. Patrick told me Jeremy shared that at the board meeting." She gave Vikki a silky smile. "Congratulations. Interesting timing, isn't it? Honeymoon baby. Such a convenient expression."

Jeremy leaped to his feet. "Hey, I don't like what you're insinuating."

Diane placed her hand above her chest. "Me, insinuating? I'm just saying the wedding was pretty sudden. After all, a man like you is a good catch." She swung her eyes toward Vikki, "Especially for some women."

As she turned away, Jeremy grabbed her arm. "What do you mean by that? You— you punk!"

Jordan jumped out of his seat, his eyes throwing daggers at Diane. "Get out of here before I forget I'm a gentleman. You sorry piece of— " Jeremy elbowed him in the side.

"That sounds like a threat," Diane said with a smirk. "Patrick will love hearing how you put your hands on me." She tossed her head and flounced off. Several people glanced at the group with questioning eyes.

After a minute of stunned silence, Jordan tapped Jeremy and raised his palms. "Work, Preacher Boy. Piece of work. Where's your faith in me, dude? At least I didn't use such a vile term as punk."

Everyone laughed, and Jeremy's mouth rose in a crooked grin, "I don't know where that came from."

Becky looked bewildered. "What's going on?"

"I'll explain later," Jessie said, gathering her composure. "Are you alright, Vikki?"

Vikki's green eyes shouted her humiliation. Jeremy wrapped his arms around his wife. "Don't worry, baby. Nobody believes any of that. Let's take a walk while the band takes a break."

"I think I'll stretch my legs, too," said Becky.

Alone with Jordan, Jessie sensed an awkwardness between them. "Well, this has been an eventful few days, hasn't it."

Jordan positioned his chair in front of Jessie. "Yeah, I'm sure you've been on an emotional rollercoaster, what with Aiden and everything." He took her hands. "Jessie, Diane put the idea of you being a burden to me in your mind, didn't she? And all that crap about me being a prince, right?"

Jessie bit her lower lip and nodded.

"And that's why you burst out about Vikki being pregnant."

Jessie covered her mouth. "I can't believe I said that, but I knew by the look on your face you were connecting the dots. I was afraid of what you might say."

"Oh, so now you're my censor?" His eyes twinkled. "Like you came up with something better."

"Well, at least it changed the subject. I feel bad for Vikki, though. I should never have said that."

"It doesn't matter. I'm sure Diane planned to make a nasty comment like that. You just gave her a great opportunity."

"Still, I wish I hadn't provided it for her."

"Oh well."

Jessie was happy to see her parents approaching them with a small cooler and camp chairs.

She waved them over. "There's room to sit here."

Jordan offered his hand to Frank. "Hi, guys. I'm glad you could make it."

Marianne gave him an obligatory smile, but Frank shook his hand. "Hello, Jordan. We've been looking forward to it. I hear there is going to be a speaker after intermission."

Jessie opened her flier, "It's a woman named Elizabeth who has paraplegia. She was treated at Hope Rehabilitation about fifteen years ago. She's going to share her story."

"That should be interesting," Frank said.

Jordan scooted his chair next to Marianne and tapped her hand. "I hear she's married."

Marianne's lips tightened in an expression Jessie knew well.

"Beautiful night for a concert, isn't it?" Jessie said, forcing her enthusiasm.

"Absolutely," Jordan said with a wink.

Jessie sighed. Hopefully, the intermission wouldn't last long. She saw a figure approaching their group from the corner of her eye. "Aiden, come here. I'm so happy you came. Sit with us. We have a blanket."

"I saw you and wanted to say hi. Um, my friends are sitting up front."

Jordan patted him on the back. "Well, we're glad you came."

Jessie introduced Aiden to her parents but didn't mention any details about their relationship other than he was a teen from church.

The band took the stage a few minutes later. Aiden excused himself to find his friends, and Jessie watched him exchange a hug with Vikki as they crossed paths. After a couple of songs, Brandon took the stage to welcome their guest.

"I'm so glad all of you gathered this beautiful evening to honor Jessie Marcus. As you all know, Jessie suffered a spinal injury in an accident a couple of months ago which left her paralyzed from the waist down."

Tingles pricked Jessie's fingers as Brandon continued. She felt as if she were hovering over her wheelchair, peering at herself below. Brandon's words explaining the purpose of the money raised echoed in the distance until they transformed into unintelligible sounds. Heat rushed to her cheeks, and the people around her morphed into waves of color. Goosebumps creeped up her arms, and she slumped forward as the colors turned gray.

Her eyes opened at Jordan's voice. "Jessie, hold on to me. Jeremy and I are going to lift you out of your chair." They lifted her smoothly and laid her on a blanket. "You blacked out for a few seconds there, Love."

Jessie wiped the sweat from her clammy face. Jordan found a water bottle, wet a napkin, and wiped her forehead. Thankfully, the incident hadn't caused much of a stir, and Jeremy reassured the few people who gathered around.

Marianne knelt beside Jessie and brushed the hair from her eyes. "Do you want to go back to the rehab center, dear?"

Jessie raised herself on one arm and paused to gain her sense of balance. "No, Mom, I'm feeling alright now. I want to hear the speaker. That's okay, isn't it?" she asked Becky, who had returned as the guys removed her from the wheelchair.

"I think so, as long as you feel well enough. Rest here for a minute. "

Jessie propped herself on her elbows as Becky had taught her. "I guess I overheated. Everything came rushing in on me."

Jordan plopped down beside Jessie and helped raise her onto his lap. "I think it was your body's reaction to stress overload. Hearing Brandon talk about the accident shook you, I'm sure. Sit here for a while until you feel stronger."

Marianne gawked at him. "Isn't she safer in her chair?"

"She's safe with me," he said, pulling her closer. "I kinda like this."

Jessie stifled a giggle. She snuggled in his strong arms wishing she could feel this way forever.

Brandon introduced Elizabeth, and the crowd grew silent as she described the fall from a ladder that left her paralyzed from the chest down. Jessie listened, filled with wonder, as Elizabeth recounted her fear, anger, and helplessness in her journey with paraplegia and how her faith in Jesus led her through the darkest moments. Jessie's skin prickled when Elizabeth said she later returned to her office job and married a man she met at work. She closed her eyes and leaned into Jordan's shoulder, absorbing the speaker's words. Elizabeth's husband didn't care that she was in a wheelchair. He had fallen in love with her after her accident. A tear trickled down Jessie's face, and Jordan tightened his embrace.

As Elizabeth made her closing remarks, Brandon approached their group and lowered himself on the blanket. "Jessie, Elizabeth would like to meet you. Would you be open to that?"

Jessie wiped her eyes and glanced at Becky. "Yes, I'd be honored, but I don't want to go on stage."

"I meant inside the church for a private chat."

"That sounds good. I know I should thank people publicly for this benefit, but I can't right now."

"No one expects that. I'll let them know you're grateful."

Vikki brought Jessie a damp tissue. "Here, your mascara smeared. This might help a little."

"I'm sure I look frightful."

Vikki wiped the mascara from under Jessie's eyes. "I'm not sure that helped much, but you look fine."

Jordan and Jeremy helped Jessie back into the wheelchair. "You're beautiful even with red eyes and mascara running down your cheeks." Jordan said.

Jessie pursed her lips. "Thanks, you know how to reassure a girl."

Marianne took a hand wipe from her purse and rubbed Jessie's cheeks, careful not to get too close to her eyes. "There, that's better."

"Well, there's a good mom." Jordan said. Marianne shot him a dark look.

Jessie wanted Jordan with her at the meeting, so they followed Brandon to a classroom in the church. Elizabeth and her husband were there waiting.

"Hello, you must be Jessie. I'm so pleased to be able to meet you."

Jessie held out her hand. "The pleasure's mine. This is Jordan."

The minister excused himself after everyone exchanged greetings. "Brandon told me about your accident when he asked me to speak," Elizabeth said. "I'm glad that you were able to attend."

"I was looking forward to the benefit but a little nervous since it's my first outing."

"I'm sure you were. There are so many 'firsts' when your life is changed in such a profound way."

"Yes, I'm finding that out. The realization of my diagnosis was overwhelming. I'm still coming to terms with it."

"Of course. It takes time. That's where my faith gave me tremendous help. Have you found that to be true?"

Jessie hesitated. She believed God never left her but didn't feel His nearness. "I'm trying to understand God's plan for me but still struggling with feelings of fear and anger. I don't see His love for me in this or how it works for my good."

Elizabeth leaned forward. "I appreciate your openness. Anger is a normal part of your emotional healing. You've faced a devastating loss. Something you could never have anticipated."

"My brother's first wife died a few years ago. I never understood how completely shattered he was until I faced my own loss. So maybe it's made me more humble. Is that what you do— try and extract some shred of purpose in it all?"

Elizabeth nodded. "I believe there's some benefit in that. But if searching for a reason is your goal, you'll never find peace. What helped me most was realizing that if my circumstances kept me from finding joy in Christ then my faith wasn't worth much. I had to walk the talk, as they say."

Jessie let out a little laugh. "You sound like my brother now. That's his goal for the church."

"I've met Jeremy. We started attending here about the time of your accident. He's a good man."

"Yes, he is." Jessie inhaled to gather courage and glanced at Elizabeth's husband. "So, you guys weren't dating before the accident?"

Elizabeth smiled and patted his knee. "No, we had only talked a couple of times."

"I always thought Elizabeth was pretty," John said, "though after losing my wife, I wasn't thinking of starting a new relationship." He put his hand on hers and grinned, "But she chased me till I gave in."

"I feel you, brother," Jordan piped up with an impish smile at Jessie.

"Oh, don't listen to John," Elizabeth said. "I resisted him because I believed I wasn't whole. I thought he deserved more. But he convinced me that my paralysis was part of me. My being in a wheelchair didn't factor into his love."

Jessie soaked in her words, and Jordan cocked his head as if to say, "See."

Elizabeth looked at her husband. Maybe you and Jordan could go for a walk. You might get some drinks if the concession stand is still open.

John seemed to take the hint. "Sure, hon. Come on, Jordan. Let's see what we can find."

Elizabeth studied Jessie for a minute. "I'm guessing Jordan is more than a friend."

"Yes, our wedding date was two weeks away before the accident, but now I don't know."

"May I ask you something personal?"

Jessie shrugged. "Sure."

"Is it Jordan who's having second thoughts? Or you?"

Jessie chewed her lower lip. "Me. Jordan wants to get married as soon as I'm released, but my parents want me to move in with them."

"And what do you want, Jessie?"

Jessie blinked back her tears. "I want to marry Jordan, but I…" She lowered her eyes. "I don't want to be a burden to him."

Elizabeth nodded and smiled softly. "You're worried about what people will think. You're worried that Jordan will tire of caring for you." She lowered her voice. "You're worried about intimacy."

Jessie met Elizabeth's eyes, "Yes, all those things."

"I felt the same way, but those worries weren't worth the energy I spent on them. For one thing, you can't control what people think or say."

"But what about the other things?"

"Jordan's love for you is evident. It emanates from his eyes as he watches you. Do you believe in his love?"

"Yes."

"I'm guessing that he knows what's involved in taking care of you."

"I'm sure he does. He's a paramedic, so that gives him more insight than most people."

"So, you can't control what others think, and you're sure of Jordan's willingness to care for you." She paused, and her eyes held a twinkle. "Trust me; you'll be able to figure out the romance."

Jessie giggled. "That's what Jordan says, the part about figuring it out."

"Sometimes you have to take a risk. It won't be an easy road, but maybe it's a journey worth taking. There are no guarantees for happiness when you walk by faith, but the promise is that God will never leave you."

Jessie gazed at this remarkable woman. "Thank you. You've opened my mind to so many possibilities. Your testimony is awesome."

"If I've given you a new perspective, that makes me happy. But you have to decide in your heart what's best for you. If you need more time to do that, then I bet Jordan will wait, don't you?"

"Yes, he's a patient man."

"Remember Jessie, your life is in God's hands. Don't fight for some misguided sense of control. Give your future to the Lord and rest in his arms."

Jessie blinked rapidly and nodded. Control was something she held tightly.

The guys returned a few minutes later and suggested it was time to return to the concert.

"Yes, I bet Becky wonders what happened to us," Jessie said. She reached out to Elizabeth for a hug. "Thanks again. For everything."

Elizabeth beamed. "Call me anytime if you want to talk. Oh, and invite me to your wedding."

Jessie grinned, and Jordan's eyes grew wide. "Um, we need to get you back, Love."

The concert was wrapping up when Jordan and Jessie returned to their spot.

"Well, they returned," Becky said with a chuckle.

"I'm sorry, Becky. I know it's late, but I need a minute with Jordan."

"No worries. I'll let him walk you to the van."

They reached the van, and Jordan lowered the ramp. Jessie rolled to the top and turned her chair to face Jordan. She took his hands. "Elizabeth and I had a nice conversation."

"That's good."

"Come closer."

Jordan dipped his head and brushed his mouth on her cheek, but Jessie turned her face and kissed his lips.

"That must have been some talk," Jordan said, drawing a deep breath.

His magnetic eyes drew her in, and the touch of his lips sent shivers down her arms. He held her face and twirled a curl around his finger. "What did Elizabeth tell you?"

Jessie touched his jaw. "We'll talk later, okay? Becky's on her way."

"Okay, Love, but you've totally wrecked me. I won't be able to sleep tonight."

CHAPTER ELEVEN

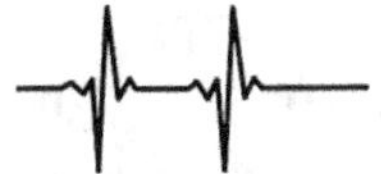

Jeremy arrived early to pray in the sanctuary, his regular practice on the Sundays he preached. He toyed with modifying his message because his actions at the benefit seemed hypocritical now. Jeremy bowed his head, "God, you know me so well." Near the end of his meditation time, Brandon entered the room.

"Sorry to interrupt, but I need to ask you something."

"I'm finished. What's up?

"Are you able to meet for a while after church?

Jeremy's stomach knotted. "Can we meet between services? I'm not teaching class."

"No, after the second service is good. I don't want to interfere with your ability to concentrate on your message.

Like he hadn't already. "Sure, is it something serious?"

"Don't worry about it. We just need to talk." He patted Jeremy's shoulder and walked away.

It was about last night. He knew it. Jeremy finished

his prayer time, considering again whether to alter his message. No, it was a good message and not enough time for changes anyway. He gathered his notes and walked to the lobby. Vikki and Heather were there waiting for him.

"Hi, guys." He knelt in front of Heather. "How's my favorite little girl?"

"Good," she said, wrapping her arms around his neck. Say hi to your favorite big girl."

Jeremy tapped her nose. "Yes, Ma'am."

He hugged Vikki. "Pray for me. I have a meeting with Brandon after church."

"About yesterday?"

"I think so. He wouldn't say."

Color crept onto Vikki's cheeks. "I knew Diane would say something. This is going to cause you trouble. I wish I hadn't gotten pregnant so soon." She looked at the floor. "I'm sorry, I don't mean that."

Jeremy led them to the lounging area close to the office and sat with Vikki and Heather on a couch. He put his arm around Vikki. "Listen, any ramifications from last night are on me. I don't think it's a big deal, anyway." He lifted Vikki's chin. "Don't ever regret this pregnancy. It's our baby, Vikki. We did nothing wrong."

Heather slid over to Vikki's lap and placed little hands on her mother's face. "Remember, Mommy, pray to Jesus when you get sad. I will help you."

"Yes, Heather, I'd like that."

Heather bowed her head. "Jesus, help Mommy to not be sad. Amen."

Vikki hugged her. "Thank you, Heather. I feel better now."

Awestruck by the blessings God continued to pour

into his life, Jeremy kissed Heather's cheek. "Let's get you to class, little prayer warrior."

It was almost time for the first service, so Jeremy and Vikki found a place near the front with enough room for Jordan if he wandered up that way. Seconds later, Jordan came strolling down the aisle, guiding Jessie's wheelchair. Jeremy froze for a second, then sprang to his feet.

"Jessie! I can't believe you're here."

"Jordan talked the doctor into letting him bring me to church."

"Without Becky?" Vikki asked. She looked at Jordan. "How did you get her here?"

"She's been practicing her transfer skills. Frank let me borrow his SUV since she's not quite ready to hop into a truck."

Jeremy tilted his head. "And Mom agreed to that?"

"Sure, Preacher Boy. I've got a way with the ladies."

Jessie raised her eyebrows. "Sorry to burst your bubble, but mom and I had a long conversation the other day. She's coming around."

Jordan grinned. "Think what you will, but you're here with me."

"There's room for your chair right here," Vikki said, "I'm so happy you came."

The service started, and Jeremy headed up the aisle during the final song. Diane and Patrick sat in their usual seats, third row on the left. Well, at least he'd get it over with. His notes stared up at him. "Be Slow to Anger." He began his message referencing several New and Old Testament verses, then focused on James 1:19-20. "Everyone should be quick to listen, slow to speak, and slow to become angry because human anger does not produce the righteousness that God desires."

Jeremy felt his usual connection with the congregation as he discussed each point. In conclusion, he brought the message home. "Some of us are relieved when we hear that verse, aren't we? We say, 'I'm off the hook with this one, God. I'm slow to anger. And when I do, it's righteous. And only to protect someone or one of your principles. I've got this.'"

Jeremy waited a beat. "Is that so? How about when people misjudge you? Or worse, insult someone you love?" He caught Diane's open-mouthed glare, and a subtle grin played around the corners of his mouth. "To be truthful, I failed at being slow to anger just hours ago." His eyes swept the hushed crowd. "We all fail in this way, don't we?"

He closed his Bible and moved to the edge of the stage. "How, then, do we become slow to anger? Most of us will never control our temper perfectly, but with God's help, we can make progress. God will help us discern when our anger is justified and not self-serving." He concluded the service, prayed and dismissed the congregation.

"What is it with you, Preacher?" Jordan said as Jeremy returned to his seat. "Am I giving you material for every sermon?"

"Nah, I think this one was for me."

"Yeah, Punk. That's awfully rough language." Jordan said with a grin.

"Apparently. It bought me a ticket to Brandon's office after church."

"Well, that should be fun. Anyway, would you guys want to come to the hospital after your talk with Brandon? Jessie thought it would be nice to have lunch in the cafeteria."

"Sure. We'll be there as soon as we can."

"Great, and don't worry. I know Brandon has your back." He looked over his shoulder as he walked away. "Just watch your mouth, huh?"

Vikki and Heather attended Sunday School and went home to wait for Jeremy. After preaching the second service, Jeremy greeted people then headed toward Brandon's office. He stopped short at the door. Patrick and Diane occupied two of three chairs that faced Brandon's desk.

Brandon looked up, "Come in, Jeremy."

"I'll come back later."

"No," Brandon said, his voice flat. "Patrick and Diane insist on being a part of our conversation."

Be slow to anger, Jeremy prompted himself and entered the office.

"Diane has made some pretty serious allegations about an incident that occurred last night. Would you like to comment?"

"Not really."

Brandon pulled his poker face, a trait Jeremy knew well. "Jeremy, Diane stated that you grabbed her arm and shouted obscenities at the benefit last night. I'd like to hear your account."

Diane stiffened. "I already told you what happened. Obviously, he has no defense."

Brandon held his hand up to Diane and turned to Jeremy with raised eyebrows. "Well?"

Jeremy shifted in his seat. "Diane insinuated that Vikki and I married quickly because Vikki was pregnant. I took a hold of her arm and turned her around. I didn't shout obscenities."

"What did you say?"

Jeremy focused on a spot over Brandon's shoulder and pressed his lips together. "I called her a punk."

Brandon's mouth twitched. "Punk?"

"Yes." Jeremy said, stifling a smile.

Diane hopped to her feet. "I'm not sure what he said, but he grabbed me. And Jordan swore at me, too! They threatened me!"

"How did they threaten you?"

"All I know is that I felt threatened. Are you going to do anything or not?"

Patrick touched his wife's shoulder. "Calm down and let Jeremy talk."

Jeremy angled his head. "I did take hold of your arm, and if you felt like it was a grab, I apologize. But nobody threatened you." He met Brandon's eyes. "I was angry. I admit calling her a name was childish. But I didn't scare her." He eyed Diane with a mocking smile. "You're not afraid of me. You're treacherous, though, and I played right into your hands."

Brandon gazed at Jeremy with parted lips. "Diane, I'd like to speak with Jeremy alone. I'll get back to you soon."

Diane's mouth gaped. "Treacherous? I just care about Vikki's reputation. And now you're making me look bad." She grabbed her husband's arm. "Patrick will take this up with the elders. He won't let you bully me." She stomped out the door with Patrick on her heels.

Brandon propped his chin on his fingers. "Well, it looks like you're in for a fight."

"Come on, Brandon. You can't believe I harmed or threatened her."

"Of course not, but Patrick is an elder. You need to watch your attitude because he can make it rough for you." He paused and averted his eyes as if trying to maintain his impassive expression. "Especially if you keep up with the name calling."

"Make it rough! He's had it in for me from the minute I accepted this position. You know that."

"I know."

"He's taking over Lee's mission to oust me."

"I understand."

"And you know Diane's going to spread gossip about the timing of Vikki's pregnancy."

"Yes."

Jeremy's fingers dug into his pant legs. "Doesn't that bother you?"

"No. Jeremy, I know your heart. I don't doubt your faithfulness or morality." He pushed back his chair. "What does bother me is Patrick's lack of support for your ministry. I've been reluctant to confront him, but this may be the turning point. I won't let him harm your reputation or the character of the church."

"I don't want to be the source of conflict. I'll resign if it comes to that."

"Absolutely not. You're the spark this church needs. You've made me a better preacher." His boyish grin lit up his face as they walked to the door. "But I'm not ready to hand over my job to you just yet."

"And I have no plans to take it. I still have a lot to learn from you."

* * *

Jessie leaned back next to Jordan on the reclining sofa in the lounge at Hope Rehabilitation Hospital. The room was empty except for the two of them.

"You're becoming a pro at transferring, Love," Jordan said, draping his arm around her shoulder. "Now are you going to tell me about your talk with Elizabeth or sentence me to another sleepless night?"

Jordan's touch threatened to melt her resolve. She closed her eyes and breathed. "Jordan, Elizabeth helped me see things more clearly." She pulled away from him. "We need to talk about us. And I want to do it before Jeremy and Vikki arrive for lunch."

Jordan sat upright. "Sure. We can do that."

"I know you love me. And you say that you don't mind caring for me." She avoided his eyes. "But what if after ten years, you get tired of it all?"

"I won't."

"How can you be certain?"

Jordan reached for her hand, but she drew it away. "Because I love you and want to care for you. I pray every night that you'll let me." He lifted her chin and met her eyes. "I've never been so sure of anything."

A lump rose in her throat. "But, what about…?"

"Jessie," Jordan ran his finger across her lower lip. "Please listen. I love you. I want to be with you. I dream about the softness of your skin, of waking up with you each morning, of loving you."

Jordan's kiss chipped away at the armor surrounding Jessie's heart. "I love you, too," she said. "But I'm afraid."

"Like I said, we can— "

"Figure it out," they said in unison. Jessie dissolved into laughter and fell into Jordan's arms.

"It'll be different for us, but we'll practice till we get it right." Jordan gazed at her with an exaggerated look of innocence, "I mean, I'll make that sacrifice."

"Oh, will you?" Jessie laughed and gave him a playful shove.

Jordan grabbed the top cushion as he fell forward. "Hey, I'd like to stay on the couch."

"And you did."

Jordan grinned and pulled himself up. "There's the spunky girl I fell in love with."

"Are we interrupting something?" Jeremy said as he and his family walked into the room.

Jordan raised his hand like a drowning victim. "Yes, rescue me, Preacher."

"Right," Jeremy said with a laugh. "Ready for lunch?"

"How did your meeting go with Brandon?" Jessie said.

"Not great. I'll fill you in while we eat."

Jeremy shared the details of his meeting during lunch. "Brandon says I'm in for a fight." He took a sip of water. "I thought it might blow over, but now I'm not so sure."

"No way is Diane going to let this go," Vikki said. "She's out for blood."

Frustration colored Jessie's face. "It's ridiculous. Patrick and Diane seem determined to get rid of you, Jeremy. Lee wanted you out because Vikki and I knew too much about his behavior toward his wife. But why do Diane and Patrick care?"

"Lee and Patrick were friends," Jeremy said, "And Patrick plain doesn't like my style of preaching."

Jordan looked at Jeremy. "Patrick voted against the board offering you the position of minister, right? He's never liked you."

"According to Vikki, Patrick thinks Lee got a bad deal on the abuse charge. He resents your involvement in bringing him to justice," Jessie said.

Vikki's phone chimed, and she frowned as she read the text. "Read this," she said, handing the phone to Jessie. "It's from Aiden."

CHAPTER TWELVE

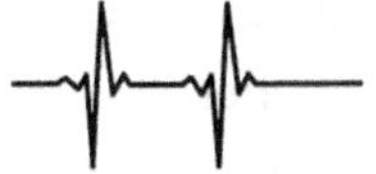

L ate Sunday afternoon, Aiden headed for the
auto shop to pick up the overflow of oil and air
filters lying around the trash bin. He'd forgotten
about the chore Friday afternoon, so he decided to stop
by to take care of it before Monday.

Since the filters wouldn't fit in the dumpster, Aiden
hauled the materials to the other trash bin in the back of
the lot. Trash poked out the top, so he moved filters, old
parts, and other junk to make room. A red piece of
nylon material caught Aiden's eye, and he tugged at it.
The fabric had twisted itself around the hinge on the
dumpster lid; he unwound it carefully and pulled. It was
a red jacket rolled around some heavy object. As he
unwrapped it, a lug wrench and pair of work gloves
tumbled to the ground. On the front of the jacket was a
patch with the words New Life Community Church.
Aiden felt an object in a zippered pocket right below the
patch and pulled out a silver keychain with some letters
engraved on the front. He squinted at the jacket in his
hands and the lug wrench lying on the ground. Why

would a lug wrench be thrown in a dumpster, and who would take time to wrap it in a jacket before tossing it?

Aiden considered his next move. As far as he knew, no one else at the shop attended New Life Community Church, and he couldn't remember seeing anyone wearing a jacket like this. He knelt beside the dumpster and wrapped up the gloves and lug wrench the way he'd found them. Maybe Vikki could help him. He trusted her, and she'd given him her number.

On the way home, Aiden stopped by the drugstore to pick up his father's medicine. On impulse, he shoved the jacket under the front seat before heading to the door. The pharmacy tech explained that it had been a busy day and that his order would be ready in about twenty minutes. As Aiden wandered down the aisles looking at nothing in particular, a jittery sensation caused him to spin around, but no one lurked nearby. He laughed under his breath. Finding that jacket must have spooked him.

A few minutes later, the tech notified Aiden the prescription was ready, and he walked to his car with his package. "What's that on my window?" he muttered. It looked like a piece of paper torn from a notebook. He pulled it out from under the wiper and flattened it. THROW THE JACKET YOU FOUND BEHIND THE TREE NEAR YOUR CAR. DON'T TELL ANYONE, OR YOU'LL BE SORRY. I KNOW WHO YOU ARE. The only tree near him was a massive oak with knobby roots pushing through the ground. He hesitated a second, then leaped into his car. Someone knew he had the jacket and had followed him to the store. Were they watching now? With trembling hands, his rattling keys found the ignition slot. His car roared to life and flew onto the road.

Aiden reached his driveway and drew in a deep breath. He sprang from the car, leaving the jacket wadded up under the seat, and dashed up the sidewalk. Then he saw it— a piece of paper taped on the front door. STAY OUT OF THIS. DON'T TALK was written in the same red ink as the other note. He yanked it from the door and stuffed it in his pocket. Aiden's blood chilled. The person following him had been to his house. Was he crouched behind some tree even now? The doorknob finally cooperated and swung open.

Once inside, Aiden managed to fix an afternoon snack for his father, who didn't seem to notice Aiden's anxiety. "If it's ok with you, I'm going to the park to meet some friends," Aiden said after chatting with his dad.

His father gave him a pointed look. "I see. When do you plan to be home?"

"I won't be gone long," Aiden said. He knew his father was still upset about his overnight excursion a few days ago and didn't fully believe his story about falling asleep in the park. "I promise, Dad. And don't worry. I've laid off the alcohol."

Aiden managed to leave the house without trouble and headed out, checking his rearview mirror. The note writer must realize he hadn't discarded the jacket by the tree. He pulled into the lot of the community park and killed the motor. He hadn't thought to bring a bag, so he stuffed the jacket under his hoodie and walked down the trail looking over his shoulder every few steps. He hoped Vikki would show up. It had taken several texts to get her to go along with his plan, and he bet she had shown the message to her friends. It wasn't until early evening that Vikki texted, agreeing to meet.

* * *

Vikki sat in the church parking lot, questioning her decision to meet Aiden. Jeremy and the others were against it. If Aiden wanted to meet, he could come to the rehab hospital they'd insisted. Aiden had refused, though. He wanted to meet with her alone, to show her something, a detail Vikki didn't tell the others. Jeremy had voiced his concern that evening as he was leaving for work.

"Vikki, you're not planning on meeting Aiden, right?" Jeremy said.

"I'm not planning on it." At least she wasn't leaning in that direction at the time.

"Don't you think it's a little strange he would ask you to meet him at the park?"

"Not really. Aiden's been through a lot. He probably wants to talk. She smiled up at her husband. "He's not dangerous."

Jeremy didn't return her smile. "Something's not right, Vikki. Amber called Jordan after we left the hospital and wanted us to come to the shop. She has information she wants to share, but not over the phone. We can't get there until Tuesday morning since we're working a long shift. I think her information might be connected with Aiden in some way."

Vikki hesitated. If Amber's news involved Aiden, he might be running scared. "Amber doesn't believe Aiden had anything to do with painting the camera lens, does she?"

"I don't know. I think it has something to do with the video footage." Jeremy held her shoulders and looked her in the eyes. "I don't want you to go, ok?"

Vikki shifted her gaze. "Well, I couldn't take Heather with me so…"

"I mean it, Vikki." He kissed her a little longer than his usual goodbye peck, and his eyes told her he was serious. "Don't go." He hugged Heather. "Be good for Mommy," he said and left for work.

Thinking back on it now, she felt a pang of guilt. Jeremy rarely told her what to do, and she hated going against his wishes. But her mom was happy to watch Heather, and Aiden's texts had sounded urgent. She stepped out of the car, hiked to the tree where she'd found Aiden a few nights ago, and sat on the creek bank.

It wasn't long before she heard footsteps, and Aiden came into view.

"Hi, there."

"I'm glad you came." Aiden looked from side to side and pulled a red jacket from his hoodie. "I wanted to show you this." He handed it to her, wrapped up as he'd found it.

Vikki unfolded the jacket and stared up at Aiden, her green eyes round with questions.

Aiden lowered his voice. "The lug wrench and gloves were wrapped inside just like that."

Vikki touched the patch with the name of the church sewn on it. "Where did you get this?"

"From a dumpster in the back of the mechanic's shop."

"New Life Community Church. That's strange. Why would it be in the dumpster where you work?"

"I don't know. Randy or Amber don't go to your church, do they? There's a keychain in the top pocket, too."

Vikki ran her fingers over the cool metal of the silver keychain. It was an ID-type chain with a space to write a name. "Do you think these letters are someone's initials? L.A.B. Look, there's a little torch beside it." She tapped the grass beside her. "Why did you want me to see these things?"

Aiden eased himself to the ground. "Look at the right sleeve."

She rubbed her fingers over the stain. "It looks like black paint. Maybe that's why someone threw it away."

"But why in our dumpster? And what about the lug wrench?"

Vikki swallowed. "You think this belongs to the person who painted the camera lens?"

"It could be. Then they loosened the lug nuts on Jessie's car." He dug in his pocket. "I've got something else to show you."

* * *

The note writer sat in his car fuming. He punched his palm with his fist. That stupid Aiden hadn't tossed the jacket under the tree. Why had the kid driven to the park? Maybe he was meeting someone to show them the jacket. The man struck his steering wheel. He shouldn't chance it, but he had to know what Aiden was up to. He thumped his head as he remembered the other entrance to the park on the edge of the church property. If he parked there, Aiden wouldn't see his car if he happened to come back to his vehicle.

As the man drove to the church, he spotted a car at the edge of the lot. Nothing to be alarmed about, people often parked there and walked down to the creek. He pulled beside the car. Blood pounded his temples when he spotted the cross hanging from the rearview mirror. Vikki's car! Was she meeting Aiden? He knew Vikki brought Aiden to the shop the other day and thought it strange. He'd only seen a glimpse of Vikki and Aiden that day before he darted back up the stairs to his office. It had been a close call.

The note writer crept toward the creek, careful not to step on fallen limbs. He froze at the faint sound of voices from a spot up the trail. Peering through the branches, he clutched a small tree trunk as fury coursed through his veins. That prying witch had been a thorn in his side from the moment he'd met her.

The man inched closer and knelt off to the side of the trail. He couldn't make out the conversation, but Aiden held the red jacket and some other small silver object he couldn't see well. Rage pulsed through his body, and he covered his mouth to keep from yelping when Aiden handed the jacket to Vikki. As if that weren't enough, Aiden pulled two pieces of notebook paper out of his pocket.

Panic seized the note writer. He crashed through the woods, abandoning the trail. They might hear the noise, but it didn't matter. He had to reach his car before Vikki noticed him. Gnarled tree roots grabbed his feet, and branches tore the skin on his sweat-drenched face. He burst out of the trees and flew toward his car. Screeching his tires, he peeled out of the lot.

Wavering between fear and rage, the man managed to drive to his apartment. He stomped inside, collapsed into his leather recliner, and massaged his aching temples. It was a coincidence he'd decided to go to the office Sunday, or he would have never seen Aiden picking up trash around the car lot. He hadn't given it much thought when the kid lugged a pile of junk to the dumpster in the back. But by some unfortunate twist of fate, Aiden had found the jacket and carried it to his car.

The man gritted his teeth. It had been stupid to hide the evidence in the dumpster, but he couldn't have anticipated some nosey brat finding it. He hoped Aiden hadn't noticed his car at the shop that afternoon. Probably not, since Aiden had entered and left from the rear of the building. His Lexus would only be in Aiden's view if he turned to look at the front lot. But these careless mistakes had to stop, or he'd ruin everything.

He knew moving back to Claymon would hold some risk, but he needed to put his life back together, and when his father offered him a job overseeing the accounts at the mechanic shop he'd recently acquired, he couldn't turn it down. Everything was working out fine until Jessie brought her car in for a tire change. The opportunity for revenge had proved irresistible. He'd laughed, thinking of her car spinning out of control as her tire wobbled loose. Jessie survived the accident as anticipated; he hadn't expected her to have serious injuries. But now he smirked at the thought of her in a wheelchair. She'd gotten what she deserved, playing him for a fool.

At first, a mechanic's error or a freak stroke of misfortune was blamed for causing Jessie's tire to loosen and snap from the car. The note writer had breathed a sigh of relief when circumstances led Aiden to accept the blame for Jessie's accident. Then out of the blue, Jordan started snooping around, trying to talk to Aiden. He thought he'd fixed that with his anonymous request for a restraining order. Of course, he knew the authorities would deny his request, but it might cause an officer to warn Jordan to back off. In a small town like Claymon, the emergency workers and police knew one another well.

The note writer dragged his hand through his

graying hair. He'd nearly come unglued the day he'd seen Jordan and that self-righteous preacher interrogating Amber. Crouching at the top of the staircase, he'd only caught enough of the conversation to know Jordan was pressing for answers. Then they had gone outside, and he could only guess they'd discovered the camera.

He'd seen Amber, Randy, and his dad huddled around the monitor the following day. They must know by now that someone had loosened the lug nuts after a mechanic parked the car in the lot. Somehow he had to keep the focus on someone at the shop, but the jacket was a colossal glitch because of the patch declaring it belonged to someone who had connections to New Life Community Church.

The note writer smacked his hands together. Well, enough was enough. At least he could work on getting rid of Jeremy. He picked up his phone, clicked a name, and typed. "Go to a place where you can talk and call me." Within a few minutes, his phone rang, and he answered. "Are you alone?"

"Of course," Diane said, her tone edgy. "I'm in a Kroger's parking lot. I made up an excuse to run to the store. What do you want, Lee?"

"I've got a snag in my plans. I'm working on it, but I may need more help from you."

"What now? I'm trying my best to ruin Jeremy's reputation, but the man is relentlessly good. He can't even swear properly. Besides, Brandon thinks he's wonderful."

"So you'll just have to work a little harder, won't you? I've got bigger problems than Jeremy's popularity. His nosy wife is more of a liability now." Lee's tone grew cold.

"Remember, you owe me."

"You agreed to keep my gambling debt out of Patrick's eyes. I'm paying you what I can. I never signed up to ruin people's lives."

"Ah, but this is part of your payment since you're low on funds. I'm still working on clearing your debt. It takes time since I have to go through old lawyer friends, and I've paid a large chunk myself. Seventy thousand is a huge amount to cover." He smiled to himself. "You know I've accepted payment in other ways."

"And look where that got me."

"That was carelessness on your part. And I fixed that, too."

Diane sniffled. "I should've known better than to get involved with you. What do you want me to do now?"

"Pull yourself together. Continue what you're doing for now. Find any little discretion and spin it to make Jeremy or Vikki look bad. Good job provoking Jeremy at the benefit, by the way. Thanks for the updates."

"But Brandon believes in Jeremy. He can do no wrong in his eyes."

"Keep the gossip going, darling. People will start to doubt. That's what matters." Lee grounded his fist in the chair arm. "Jeremy and his friends have to go. They've taken too much from me."

He sugared his voice. "Remember, Diane, we know many secrets about each other. You're stuck with me, but that's not too bad. We can run away together if it gets too heated."

He disconnected and reached for the bottle of whiskey he kept near the chair. As much as he wanted Jeremy out of the picture, Aiden and Vikki were his biggest concern. He lifted the bottle to his mouth. A few swigs would ease his throbbing head.

CHAPTER THIRTEEN

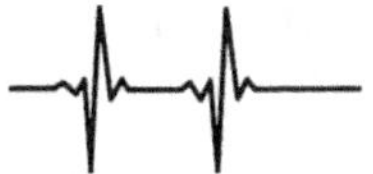

After his shift Tuesday morning, Jeremy drove home before meeting with Amber. Heather met him at the door, and he swept her above his head, swinging her around like an airplane.

"I'm flying," she giggled. He lowered her, and she squealed, "More, Daddy! Make me fly more."

He lifted her again, then swayed back and forth, finally placing her on the ground. "Where's Mommy?"

"Taking a shower."

Jeremy sat on the floor and helped Heather work on a puzzle. "Well, what did you do yesterday?'

"Went to Gran and Gramps' house."

"Did you and Mommy have fun there?"

"Mommy didn't go," Heather answered without looking up.

Jeremy let the puzzle piece hover over its place. "Why didn't Mommy go?"

"She had erwans."

"Really?" Jeremy could place bets on the errand she'd

run. He tousled Heather's hair. "I think I'll see if Mommy's done with her shower."

He met Vikki in the hallway wearing jeans and a t-shirt with a towel wrapped around her head. Her emerald eyes were huge. "Oh!"

"Hi. Sorry, I didn't mean to scare you."

Vikki pointed to the bedroom door, motioning for Jeremy to follow her. "I need to tell you something."

"Uh, huh."

Vikki held the cross on her necklace, and the color rose in her cheeks. "I met with Aiden yesterday."

"Yeah, how about that?"

"What?"

"Heather told me she stayed with Gran while you ran erwans. It wasn't difficult to figure out."

"Are you angry?"

Jeremy paused; he was more surprised than angry, he supposed. "I asked you not to go." Dang, those green eyes— always messing with him. He pulled the towel off her head and tucked a strand of wet hair behind her ear. "I'm not mad, just curious why you felt you had to meet Aiden even though I didn't want you to."

"I'm sorry. I wasn't going to, but Aiden's texts seemed urgent." She met Jeremy's eyes. "I want you to see what he gave me." She pointed to a bundle on the bed. "Open it."

Jeremy unwrapped the bundle, turning each piece in his hands before laying it back on the bed. He met Vikki's eyes. "Where did Aiden get these things?"

Uneasiness washed over Jeremy as Vikki filled in the details. "What do you make of all this?" she asked.

Jeremy picked up the half sheets of paper. "I don't know, but these notes are definitely threatening." He brushed his bangs back. "Does Aiden have any idea who wrote them?"

"No, but we think it's the same person who owns the jacket." She looked at Jeremy. "I mean, don't you? Did you notice the black paint on the sleeve?"

"Yes, and the owner of the jacket is probably the one who painted the camera lens."

"And loosened the lug nuts."

Jeremy shrugged. "That would be my guess." He ran his fingers over the badge on the jacket. "But I can't figure out the connection with the church."

"Me either. I don't know anyone at Amber's shop who's ever been to New Life."

"Except Aiden."

"Oh, Jeremy. You can't believe he had anything to do with it."

"No, it couldn't be Aiden's. The church sold those jackets at least five years ago. He would have been a kid."

"Then I don't get it. Who would be out to get Jessie?"

Jeremy drew in his breath. He didn't want to voice his thoughts. "I've seen Patrick wearing a jacket like that."

"Why would Patrick want to harm Jessie? Unless he thought it would hurt you."

Jeremy frowned. The elder made no bones about his feelings regarding him, but he didn't think Patrick would stoop that low. "I don't think so, even though he'd love to get rid of me. Hurting Jessie doesn't make sense. And the initials on the keychain aren't his."

Vikki put the keychain back in the jacket pocket and wrapped the jacket around the tool and gloves. "What do we do with this? I have a picture of it on my phone."

Jeremy reached for the bundle. "I want to show it to Jordan before our meeting with Amber." He took Vikki's hands. "Promise me you won't meet Aiden alone again. You both could be in danger." He glanced at the slight bulge on her stomach. "And please remember that you have our baby to think about."

She touched her midsection, and pink invaded her cheeks. "I know. But what if he texts?"

"Then call me. I'll contact Officer Trent to let him know what Aiden found and the threatening notes."

"That's a good idea."

Jeremy said his goodbyes to Heather, then took Vikki in his arms. "Please be careful and stay away from secluded places like the park. You hear me?"

"Yes, Jeremy. You already told me that."

Jeremy raised his eyebrows. "Yeah, like that matters."

Vikki's green eyes flashed. "I'm not a child."

He held back a smile. "I know, baby. I'm worried about you. That's all."

* * *

Jeremy met Jordan in the parking lot and showed him Aiden's discovery, explaining Vikki's meeting with Aiden.

"Unbelievable! What do you think about it?"

"I don't know, but it looks like whoever tampered with Jessie's car has connections with New Life Church."

"Who could that be? I doubt Amber or Randy ever went there. Aiden goes, but he's the one that found the jacket."

"I thought about Patrick, though that seems like a stretch."

"Yeah, the guy doesn't exactly adore you, but what would he have against Jessie?" Jordan's face took on a look of realization. "Wait a minute. I wonder if he knew Jessie called Lee's wife after their little fling. He might think he was doing Lee a favor by hurting Jessie."

"Exactly, but it still seems far-fetched."

"Yeah. We'd better go in and find out what Amber has for us. Do you think we should keep the jacket under wraps for now?"

"Yes. Wait a second. I'll put it in my car."

Amber met them at the door and led them to the front desk. Only a few people were in the waiting area, and Randy was assisting a customer at the counter. "I want you to see something," she said.

She entered a password on the computer keyboard. Jeremy and Jordan looked over her shoulders. "This is a history of the camera video." She pointed to the screen. "Look, here's when the camera you looked at stopped recording. It was the night before Jessie picked up her car."

Jeremy studied the screen. "So that's when the lens was painted black?"

Amber looked from Jeremy to Jordan. "Yes, but, interestingly, the cameras were turned off for about twenty minutes during the same time period."

Jeremy's heart raced, and he caught his breath. "Then that means someone spray painted the lens while none of the cameras were recording."

"But that doesn't make sense," Jordan said. "If someone had access to the security system, why bother painting the lens black?"

"I don't know. Maybe to throw people off the track? We thought the camera wasn't working. Someone painting the lens never crossed our minds."

Jordan looked up. "The guy who did this probably thought no one would bother studying the video footage if they discovered the painted lens. And if they didn't find the painted lens, they'd think it was a malfunctioning camera."

"That's what I think," Amber said. "Even if someone discovered that the cameras had been turned off, there would be no evidence. And the plan worked until you started asking questions."

Randy finished with his customer and walked over to the computer desk. "What do you think about all of this?" he said.

Jeremy met his gaze. "I think someone who has access to the security system wanted to harm Jessie."

"But that's crazy, man. Only a few people have access to the system."

"Right," Jordan said. "And who are these people?"

Randy squared his shoulders. "What are you trying to say? Do you think I did it?"

Jordan returned his stare." I'm not accusing anyone. But we need to know who could have done it. Do any mechanics have the ability to shut off the security cameras?"

"No, but I guess one of them could have painted the camera lens black. And the cameras may have glitched at the same time."

"That would be an unlikely coincidence," Jeremy said.

Amber spoke up. "You're right. It would be. And the only people that have the code to turn the cameras off are Ben, Randy, and myself."

"And Aaron," said Randy.

"Oh, I forgot about him. Aaron is Ben's son. But he wouldn't know Jessie."

Jeremy ran his fingers through his hair. "That means someone here…" he caught the exchange between

Amber and Randy. "What do we know about the owner and his son? Do they go to New Life Community Church?"

Amber's eyes held questions. "I don't think so, why?"

Jordan gave Jeremy an open-mouthed gaze, "Well then. I guess we're bringing the jacket in after all."

Jeremy lifted his palms. "We might as well. I'll get it."

Jeremy returned with the jacket, and Amber suggested they move to the conference room while Randy stayed at the counter to oversee the shop. After examining the items, Amber confirmed the lug wrench and gloves could be from the shop. "How about the keychain?"

Jeremy said. "Have you ever seen it?"

She turned it over in her hand. "No. Do you think these are initials?"

"Possibly," said Jordan. "If so, it would clear you and Randy. How about your boss and his son?"

Amber's cheeks reddened, and she glanced away. "Aaron and Ben wouldn't fit the initials either." She stood abruptly. "This is all very interesting, but I have a shop to run. Maybe you should call the police. I don't want to get involved."

Jordan narrowed his eyes. "It's a little late for that. Someone in this shop knows something."

Jeremy snatched the jacket. "Amber's right. We'll be in touch." He took Jordan's arm.

"Let's go and let Amber take care of her business."

"Why the sudden exit, Preacher? We need to find out more about the owner of this place," Jordan said as they walked to their vehicles.

"Did you see Amber's face? She's hiding something."

"Like what?"

Jeremy shrugged. "I don't know, but she knows something, or else she's afraid of someone who does."

* * *

Jessie spotted Vikki and Heather coming toward the cafe. "Hi, guys. I'm glad you could come for lunch." She took the picture the little girl held out to her. "Thank you, Heather. What a pretty flower."

Heather pointed to the space under the picture. "I made my name. And I have art things in my bag."

The letters forming her name were typical of a preschooler's carefully drawn scrawls and scribbles. "That's fabulous. I'm so proud of you." Jessie pulled her into a hug. "It's been a long time since I've seen you. What do you want to eat?"

Since it was a nice day, they took their lunch to the courtyard picnic table near the fountain. Colorful flowers in full bloom perfumed the air with their sweet aroma. Heather played with the markers, paper, and other supplies while the grown-ups talked.

Jessie's stomach knotted as Vikki told her about her meeting with Aiden and what he'd found. "Are you saying that someone loosened my wheel on purpose?" The look in Vikki's eyes answered her question.

"That's the only thing Aiden and I could think of. I showed it all to Jeremy and he agreed with us." Vikki scrolled through her pictures and handed the phone to Jessie. "I took a picture of the jacket and tools. There was a keychain with some lettering on it in the pocket. I didn't get a picture of it because we thought we heard someone coming."

Jessie's shaking fingers enlarged the photos. She had an odd feeling that she'd seen the jacket before. "So, these jackets were sold to church members several years ago?" She further enlarged the photo to read the words on the patch. "It seems like I've seen it somewhere."

"People still wear them occasionally. Jeremy said all the board members and elders got one. Brandon wears his at times, and I saw one or two being worn at the benefit concert."

Jessie closed her eyes for a moment. "I feel it wasn't in the church where I saw it."

"You could have seen a jacket like it anywhere around Claymon. A lot of people attend New Life."

"Hmm, I guess so. I hadn't spent much time in Claymon before I met Jordan. Does he know about this?"

"I'm sure he does by now. Jeremy took the jacket to show Jordan this morning before they met with Amber."

Jessie's head throbbed. "I chose to believe the accident was some freak happening, especially after we found out it wasn't a mechanic's mistake. Now I don't know what to think."

Vikki touched her shoulder. "I'm sorry, Jessie. I didn't mean to upset you."

"Don't be sorry. I need to know." Jessie rested her jaw on her hand. "I can't think of anyone at church that doesn't care for me except Diane, and that's just because I'm Jeremy's sister. I can't imagine she'd actually hurt me."

"I know, but remember, Lee was Patrick's friend. Maybe Patrick's out to avenge him."

Jessie choked back a laugh. "Are you saying straight-laced Patrick loosened the lug nuts?"

Vikki grinned, but her eyes were uneasy. "I know it sounds nuts." She drew in a breath and put her hand over her mouth. "Wait! I saw one of those jackets in the conference room closet at church. Some of the board members and elders store things in it. Jeremy said the jacket I saw belonged to Patrick."

"So?"

"So, if it isn't there now, the jacket Aiden found might belong to Patrick."

Jessie leaned back in her chair. "So, what's your plan to find out if Patrick's jacket is missing? And if it is, that's not proof of anything."

"I can look in the closet. If it is there, then Patrick's off the hook."

"What if someone sees you?"

"I'm at the church a lot. No one will think anything of it. If I need to, I can get in with the code."

"And you think Jeremy is going to go along with this?"

Vikki hesitated. "If I leave right now, I won't have to worry about Jeremy's opinion."

CHAPTER FOURTEEN

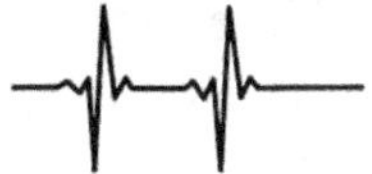

A s Vikki pulled into the church lot, she recognized Brandon's truck and the secretary's SUV. The few other vehicles around belonged to maintenance and tech people. She paused for a minute, exited the car, and opened Heather's door.

"Are we taking Daddy his lunch?"

"No, not today. Daddy's working from home," Vikki said as she scoped the lot again. She didn't anticipate Jeremy being at the church, but he might need to stop by for a meeting or to pick something up. She'd have to move quickly.

"Come in," a voice said after she rang the doorbell.

The secretary greeted them, and Vikki explained that she needed to look for something in the office. It wasn't a lie. "I'll only be a minute."

"Sure."

Vikki smiled and started down the hallway. The furniture in the conference room consisted of a long table with padded chairs arranged around it. Several pictures of people engaging in church activities adorned the walls, and a potted philodendron graced the table. A clasp envelope with "Benefit Funds" written across the front lay propped on the plant's container. Someone must have mistakenly left it after a meeting since it contained donations for Jessie's medical expenses. Vikki shoved it inside Heather's backpack so she could hand it to the secretary on her way out.

She walked to the closet and pushed through hangers holding a few jackets and other church apparel. Then she spotted a red jacket. It was Patrick's alright; the tag inside the neck had his name written on it. She returned the coat to the closet and picked up Heather's bag.

Vikki jumped at the sound of a voice behind her, "What are you doing here?"

She spun around. Diane stood there with a sneer on her face. Vikki stepped back and reached for Heather. "I just came to look for something in the closet."

Diane gaped at the backpack. "What are you doing with that envelope?'

"I found it on the table. It has money inside. I'm giving it to Nan on my way out.

"That's interesting. You came all the way here to look in the closet, and you just happened to find an envelope with money?" Diane reached for the envelope, but Vikki snatched it. Diane's face reddened, and her brows furrowed in a V shape. "Give it to me!"

"What's the matter with you?" Vikki said, clutching the package to her chest. I told you I'm taking it to Nan."

At that moment, Brandon poked his head into the room. "May I help you, ladies?"

Jeremy stood peering over Brandon's shoulder. "Vikki? What are you doing here?" He pushed around the pastor and gathered Heather, who clung to Vikki's leg, in his arms. What's going on?"

"I can tell you," Diane said before Brandon shut the door. I caught Vikki stealing the benefit money."

"What!? I found it on the table." Vikki said, and she met Jeremy's astonished eyes. "I was planning to turn it in at the front desk."

Brandon cleared his throat. "Let's all sit down and discuss this calmly."

Diane crossed her arms. "Patrick sent me to pick up the money so I could take it to the bank and make the deposit." She flashed a saccharine smile. "You're aware that I do that for him sometimes, since he handles the money around here."

"No, I'm not aware of that," said Brandon. "Go on."

"Well, I do. Anyway, I came in here and found Vikki snooping around in the closet with the money in her hand. She panicked when I caught her."

Vikki blinked back tears and sharp tingles ran down her arms. Jeremy held Heather on his lap staring at her.

Brandon spoke quietly. "Vikki, can you tell us what you were doing in this office?"

"I found the envelope like I told you. I was going to give it to Nan on the way out because I thought someone left it here by mistake." Her eyes drilled into Diane's. "I wasn't stealing, and it wasn't in my hand."

Diane leaned across the table. "So, why were you here snooping around?"

Brandon's face held questions as he looked at Vikki.

Vikki averted her gaze. "I was looking for something."

"Of course," Diane said, "the benefit money."

Jeremy rose from his seat. "That's enough, Diane."

Vikki grasped the table edge, never wanting to slap someone so much in her life. "I wasn't taking the money," she spat out. She grabbed her purse. "Come on, Heather."

Jeremy caught her arm. "Wait a minute, Vikki," he said, turning toward Brandon, "Can we talk to Vikki alone?"

Brandon stood. "Diane, would you please excuse us?"

"What? Are you going to take her word over mine? She's the one who was snooping around in the closet with the money in her hand."

Brandon looked at her with steady eyes. "We've heard your story, so we need to talk to Vikki now. And I'll take care of the money." Vikki handed him the envelope.

"I'm supposed to take that," Diane said and grabbed for the envelope, but Brandon had it in a firm grip.

"I'll take care of it. Goodbye, Diane." Brandon escorted her to the door.

She stomped her foot and glared at him. "I'm telling Patrick about this. You'd better find out what Vikki was doing with the money in her hand, or you might be looking for another church!"

Brandon shut the door behind Diane. "Whoo!" He walked back to the table. "Vikki, will you tell us what you were looking for in the closet?"

Vikki touched her necklace, searching for a reasonable answer. Brandon's lips formed a straight line on his expressionless face. She couldn't bring herself to look at Jeremy.

"Vikki," Brandon said slowly, "I'm not accusing you of anything. But I need something to go on. Diane's not going to let this drop."

Vikki knew Brandon deserved an explanation. "I was looking for one of Jeremy's jackets. I thought he might have left it here." She glanced at Jeremy. His gaze told her he recognized the lie in her eyes.

Brandon rested a finger on his lips. "In that closet? Jeremy never puts his things in there."

"Well, I thought he might."

"Alright," Brandon said with an expression that told Vikki he doubted her story. "It doesn't matter anyway. The money is safe, and I'll get Patrick to deposit it."

Jeremy carried Heather to Vikki's car and buckled her in. "I guess I'll see you later," he said. He gave her a puzzled look. "I have some things to take care of here."

"I'm sorry, Jeremy. I had this great idea, but it didn't work out."

"Uh huh," Jeremy lifted her chin. "We'll talk it out later, okay? Right now, I think you and Heather need to go home and unwind." He brushed a strand of hair from her face and angled his head. "For the record, you shouldn't lie. You're rotten at it."

"Bye." Vikki said. She would have a lot of explaining to do this evening.

Vikki spent the afternoon working around the house. She decided to grill hamburgers for supper and climbed the stairs to the furnished apartment above her house, bringing Heather along to play as she prepared the evening meal. A smile tipped the corners of her mouth at the thought of the first time she met Jeremy when he came to inquire about her ad in the paper. The decision to rent him the apartment had changed her life.

When Jeremy texted he was on the way home, Vikki let him know her plans for supper. Jeremy climbed the stairway and opened the door that led to the kitchen. "We haven't eaten on the balcony for a while. Is this a diversion tactic?"

Color rose on Vikki's cheeks. "Maybe. Go play with Heather while I finish up."

Jeremy smiled. "Sure, baby. I'll deal with you later."

Vikki swatted him with a towel, and he grabbed it from her hand.

"You better watch it, girl. You're in enough trouble," he said and tossed the towel back to her.

* * *

It wasn't until after Heather was asleep that Jeremy brought up the afternoon's events. "Are you ready to talk to me?"

Vikki closed the book she was reading and looked at him from her perch on the living room chair. "I guess so."

Jeremy sat on the couch. "What were you looking for in the closet?"

"Patrick's New Life Community jacket."

"Patrick's jacket? Why?" He gazed at her for a long second. "You mean to see if the red jacket Aiden found could be Patrick's? Don't you think that was a little risky?"

"It would have been fine if Diane hadn't shown up."

"But she did. Who knows what she'll do next."

Vikki's eyes snapped. "I know. She'll spread it all around the church and make me look like a thief. I wish I could smack her upside the head." Jeremy brought his hands to his lips as if smothering a smile. She glared at him. "I don't know what you find so amusing about this."

Jeremy looked away for a second, then grinned at her. "I'm just imagining the scene of you attacking Diane. Sorry."

Unexpected hilarity bubbled inside Vikki as Brandon's confused face and Jeremy's look of shock that afternoon replayed in her mind. At the image of Diane stomping her feet, she doubled over in giggles. "Oh, Jeremy, what have I done?" she said, gasping for breath.

"I don't know, but I wish I had a picture of your eyes when you jumped up from that table," Jeremy said, laughing. "And the look on Brandon's face was priceless."

Vikki wiped her eyes. "What did Brandon say after I left?"

"Don't worry, baby," Jeremy said, catching his breath. "Brandon doesn't believe you had any intentions of stealing the money, and he even bought that ridiculous story about looking for my jacket. Or at least he let it go."

Vikki bristled. "Well, I was looking for a jacket, so it wasn't a complete lie. There's one thing I can't figure out. Why would Patrick leave the benefit money on the table for Diane to pick up instead of taking it to the bank?"

"He didn't leave it for Diane." Jeremy leaned forward. "Get this. Brandon told me he found the money lying under papers on my desk when he was looking for a book he'd loaned me."

Vikki wrinkled her eyes. "That doesn't make sense. How did it get on your desk, and who put it on the conference table?"

"We have no idea how the money got on my desk, but Brandon decided to put it on the table in the conference room for Patrick to pick up and deposit since we had a meeting scheduled there early this evening." He sat back on the couch. "Nobody expected you to find the money, or Diane to come looking for it."

A knot formed in Vikki's gut. Was someone trying to

set Jeremy up? "Maybe the custodian found it while cleaning and put it on your desk."

Jeremy looked skeptical. "I guess. Though I'd think she'd take it to the front office and give it to Nan."

"Diane probably persuaded her lame husband to put it there to frame you. Or she did it herself."

Jeremy's lips rose a bit. "You're awfully feisty. Where's my sweet, shy girl who always looks for the best in people?" He pushed his bangs to the side. "Though, I should listen to you since it was your determination that brought Lee's true colors to light. You put yourself in danger to help his wife."

Vikki moved to the couch. "You believed me and helped me figure out what to do. I love you for that."

Jeremy looked at her. "Do you really think Patrick had anything to do with Jessie's accident?"

"No, I guess not since it wasn't his jacket that Aiden found."

Jeremy draped his arm around Vikki's shoulders. He told her about his and Jordan's visit with Amber at the shop. "Someone there is either guilty or knows something, and we're going to find out who it is. Jordan plans to work on his house this evening, though, 'cause he wants to take Jessie to see it tomorrow."

"They're going to let Jordan take her from the rehab center?"

"You know Jordan. He's dazzled the whole staff."

Vikki giggled. "I'm sure that's true." She hoped Jessie would be pleased with the idea.

"Jordan wants to show Jessie the jacket so she's in the loop, and he'd like for us to be there," Jeremy said.

"By the way, Heather and I visited Jessie this morning," Vikki said. "I showed her pictures of the jacket. She's having difficulty accepting that someone intentionally caused her wreck."

"Letting her see the pictures was a good idea. She'll have time to think it through before seeing the actual jacket."

"Should we call the police? Is Aiden in danger?"

"I'm not sure. Aiden no longer has the jacket, but we don't know if the person who wrote the notes knows that. Jordan talked to Officer Trent, and he agreed to keep Aiden on his radar and see that his street is patrolled."

Jeremy stood up, pulling Vikki with him. "Maybe Mom could watch Heather tomorrow morning while we talk to Jessie. She took a few days off."

Vikki stretched. "Okay. I'm pretty tired."

Jeremy took her in his arms and kissed her forehead. "No, wonder. Sleuthing is hard work."

CHAPTER FIFTEEN

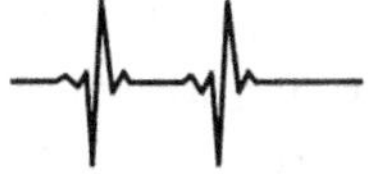

Jessie waited in the foyer, tapping a rhythm on her wheelchair arm. Physical and occupational therapists had taken her on several outings to teach her the intricacies of navigating a world she now saw in a much different light. This day, however, was her first venture without a therapist. Jordan had borrowed his stepdad's SUV and convinced the staff that she was ready for an outing with friends. He wanted to show her the renovations on his house and promised to have her back within a couple of hours. Now she waited with a mixture of excitement and hesitancy. Spotting Jordan's swagger and easy smile as he walked through the door, she waved him over.

His eyes lit up as he approached. "Hi, Love. Ready for our big adventure?"

They went through the process of checking her out and headed to the parking lot. She wheeled up to the door and, without much help from Jordan, transferred into the seat and took one of the wheels off her chair.

"Hey, you're getting good at this," Jordan said as he removed the other wheel and put them and the chair in the back.

Jessie glowed with pride. "I've learned so much these past few weeks. I feel stronger every day."

"That's wonderful, Love." Jordan hopped in the SUV and squeezed her hand.

The comfortable feeling of anticipation when arriving home from a long journey filled Jessie as Jordan turned into the driveway of his white farmhouse, sitting on an acre lot a few miles north of Claymon. The scent of trumpet honeysuckle with its bright red flowers floated in the air as Jordan helped her transfer from the SUV.

Jessie inhaled. "What a delicious aroma."

"Thanks to my mom," Jordan said. "She says every house should be adorned with a beautiful flower garden."

"Well, they are beautiful. She did a fabulous job."

"Wait till you see inside."

Jessie wheeled up the newly formed sidewalk sloping up to the front entrance. Jordan opened the door, and she caught her breath at the sight of the beautiful wood floor. He led her to the kitchen decked out with wheelchair-accessible cabinets and countertops, then took her down the hallway to his remodeled bedroom with a widened door and identical wood flooring as the rest of the house. But the scene that brought tears to her eyes was the bathroom. It was spacious enough to maneuver her chair and had a handicapped-accessible shower. She looked at Jordan with wonder. "I can't believe the amount of work you've done. It's amazing."

Jordan beamed. "I'm glad you liked it, but I didn't do nearly all of this. A lot of people worked long hours to finish it. We have a couple of builders in the congregation. Everyone has been so generous." He took her hand. "It's all for us, Jessie. That's when, or if," his voice trailed off.

Jessie blinked away the tears forming in her eyes. "It's too much, Jordan. I don't deserve all this."

"Of course you do, Jessie. What you didn't deserve was some maniac tampering with your car causing you to end up in a wheelchair."

Jessie's eyes welled with tears. "I don't know. I wasn't living right when I met you."

Jordan wheeled her into the living room and up to the oversized sectional he'd inherited from his parents. It was a soft gray color with recliners at both ends. "Let's sit on the couch, okay?"

Jessie positioned her chair, pushed off with her hands, and swung her hips onto the couch while Jordan helped steady her. She smiled through tears, "I am getting better, aren't I?"

"Yes, Love," Jordan said as he slid beside her. He hesitated as if searching for words, "Jessie, do you think your accident was some kind of punishment from God?"

Jessie shuddered at the memories of who she'd been before Jordan came into her life. "I wasn't living like I'd been taught when we met. I was never a promiscuous party girl, but I made poor choices— not the kind good Christians make."

"We've been through that, Love. Everyone makes mistakes. We've traveled different roads, so my failures aren't the same as yours. But in God's eyes, your sins are no worse than mine, or anyone else's." He turned her face to his. "Don't you believe that your sins are forgiven?"

"Yes, but... I can't help thinking I'm being punished.

Don't you agree there are consequences for your actions?"

"Sure, and we all live with them, but sometimes bad things happen for reasons we don't understand. I don't think we're protected from tragedy because we're good Christians. Look at your brother. His first wife, beaten and murdered while he lay bleeding. She did nothing to bring that on." Jordan wrapped his arms around her. "I don't think God is punishing you, Jessie. But I do think God brought us together for a reason."

"Yes, but it all seems blurry now, doesn't it? You didn't sign up for this. You know, I mean, caring for someone disabled like me."

"I didn't sign up for anything. I fell in love." Jordan's eyes sparkled. "If I saw you for the first time today, I'd have the same rush I had the day we met. If you say yes, we'll have Jeremy perform the ceremony when he gets here, and I'll never take you back to the hospital."

"They'd come after me, and Becky would have your head."

Jordan laughed. "Yeah, you're right. I think she could take me down."

Jessie snuggled close to Jordan, and her heart swelled with love. She'd never understand his complete acceptance of her and all her baggage, but she finally let her mind believe what her heart had always known. Jordan wanted her because of who she was—headstrong, imperfect, and in a wheelchair. She touched his cheek. "Okay."

"Okay, what?"

"Okay, I'll marry you." She yawned. "Probably not tonight, though. I'm kinda tired."

Jordan stared at her. "Don't tease me, Jessie."

She giggled, her amber eyes glowing. "I'm not. I mean about marrying you if you still want me."

Jordan looked as if he couldn't believe her words. "If I still want you?" He ran his finger across her cheek. "You know I do. I love you, Jessie." He popped up the recliner and pulled her onto his lap.

His kiss took her breath away. "I love you too, Jordan."

He kissed her again, his hands running through her hair and caressing her shoulders.

"Hey," he said, lowering the recliner and scooting her off his lap, "Jeremy and Vikki should be here soon. I invited them to see the house."

Jessie raised her eyebrows and tilted her head. "Oh? You don't trust yourself alone with me?"

He twisted a stray curl around his finger. "It's not me I'm worried about."

Jessie snickered. "Right, you're just so irresistible."

Jordan raised his palms and grinned. "Yeah, it's the thorn in my side, but I deal with it." His eyes misted, "Seriously, though, I've prayed for this every day. I don't want to live without you."

"I'm sorry, Jordan. I'm sorry I ever doubted you."

"It's all good, Jessie. You needed time."

Jessie leaned her head on his shoulder, letting the peace that had eluded her for so long flood her soul.

After a few minutes, Jordan broke the silence. "Jeremy and Vikki are going to show you something Aiden found when they get here."

"I know about the jacket. Vikki visited me yesterday and showed me pictures she'd taken with her phone."

"I didn't know that. Well, what did you think?"

"I don't know what to think. Vikki believes it might

be Patrick's jacket. She planned on going to the church to see if she could find it in some closet."

"Why? Jeremy didn't say anything about that."

"To rule Patrick out. Jeremy didn't know. He might now, though. I haven't heard from Vikki."

There was a rustling at the door, and the bell rang. "Come in," Jordan called from the couch.

"Ooh, the floor is beautiful," Vikki said, scanning the room. She eyed Jessie with surprise. "You're on the couch."

"Yes, it's good to be out of the chair." Jessie patted Jordan's knee. She wondered how long he could keep quiet about their wedding plans.

Jordan stood to meet them. "Hi, guys. You'd better brush up on your wedding ceremony, Preacher. She finally roped me into it."

Jeremy and Vikki exchanged stunned glances. Vikki skipped to the couch and embraced Jessie.

"That's wonderful. I'm so happy for you both."

Jeremy punched Jordan on the arm. "No kidding. Congratulations!"

"Yeah well, a man can only take so much begging before he breaks." Jordan winked and tousled Jessie's hair.

Jessie laughed. "You're irrepressible, you know that?"

Jordan winked. "I've heard rumors."

They talked about wedding plans for a few minutes, then Jordan and Jessie took them on a house tour. Vikki and Jeremy marveled at the changes.

Jordan thanked them. "You both had a part in this, too."

After touring the house, they returned to the living room, and Jeremy picked up a bag he'd dropped by the door. "We wanted you to see these, Jessie," he said, placing the rolled-up jacket on her lap. He took a chair close to Jessie. "I know Vikki showed you pictures, but we thought you needed to see the real thing."

Jessie unrolled the bundle. She gripped the lug wrench, the metal heavy in her hand. The tool mechanics utilized to ensure people's safety had wielded destruction by another's hand. "Why? Who would do this to me?"

Jordan stroked her arm. "That's what we're trying to find out." He told her about the conversation with Randy and Amber, including the part about all the cameras being turned off for twenty minutes the night before she came to pick up her Mustang.

"Somebody in that shop knows something." Jeremy added, his face grim.

Vikki pointed to the jacket. "The keychain I didn't get a picture of is in the top pocket."

Jessie drew her lips together as she held the keychain. The initials L.A.B. stared back at her. She gasped when she spotted the torch etched near the letters.

Vikki knelt beside her wheelchair. "Jessie, what is it?"

All eyes focused on the keychain in Jessie's hand. She moved her mouth, forming words that came out in breathless spurts. "That torch by the initials is the symbol for the law firm where— where Lee Bannister worked. Lawyers and some of the other employees had that torch etched into their jewelry." Her raspy voice echoed inside her ears. She cupped them with her hands, and the keychain fell to her lap. "L.A.B.— Lee Bannister. I don't know his middle name, but this must belong to Lee."

Jordan jumped to his feet. "So, Lee's still after you.

But how would he have known your car was in Amber's shop?"

"Hey, wait a second," Vikki said. "Whoever wants that jacket knows Aiden found it. It was Lee! He must have seen Aiden digging in the dumpster."

Jeremy ran his hand across his forehead. "But why would he be at the shop?" He paused as if turning something over in his mind. "Aaron. The owner's son's name is Aaron."

Jordan's mouth fell open. "Jeremy, remember the time we saw a man walking in the shop as we were leaving. We both thought he looked familiar but couldn't place him. That's because he looked like Lee, but older. Could he be Lee's father?"

"You're right. We assumed he was the shop owner."

Jessie looked at her brother. "What's the owner's last name?"

"Amber always just says Ben and refers to his son as Aaron. But Lee could be using his middle name."

Vikki pulled out her phone. "I have Aiden's number, maybe he knows Ben's last name."

Aiden answered her text quickly. Vikki read it out loud. "I'm at work. Give me a minute and I'll try to find out."

Jordan pulled out his phone. "Why wouldn't he know? I'll give him a few minutes, 'cause I bet we can google the name of the store to find out who owns it."

Jessie thought about her time working with Lee and her terrible mistake in getting involved with him. "He's still trying to get back at me for calling his wife. I was such a fool."

Vikki patted her hand. "You thought he was divorced. He lied to you, Jessie. Everyone makes mistakes."

"Yes, but the repercussions of this one…" A tear leaked from the rim of her eye.

Jordan turned toward her. "Jessie, don't. Don't go back to dark places. We'll get through this together."

Vikki's phone chimed, and she read the text aloud. "The owner's name is Benjamin Bannister."

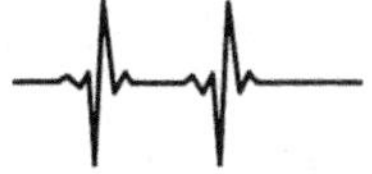

CHAPTER SIXTEEN

"Can I help you with something?"

Aiden pushed the send arrow and shoved his phone in his pocket. He stared into the face of the man who loomed over him." No. I, uh, I was just looking around."

Ben Bannister's face held a mixture of doubt and irritation. "In my office?"

Aiden willed his feet not to propel him out of the room. "I just peeked in to see whose office it was."

Ben's brow wrinkled. "Aren't you supposed to be downstairs working?"

"Yep, I'd better get back to work." Aiden darted down the steps. Swearing to himself for being so careless, he waited for Mr. Bannister to come looking for him. The shop door wasn't far, but running wouldn't help his situation. He turned his attention to the vehicle assigned to him.

Aiden checked the oil level and replaced the cap. The corner of his eye caught a figure coming toward him. He strolled over to chart his work as if he wasn't aware of her approach.

"Aiden, I need to see you for a minute."

He took a deep breath and put on the most natural expression he could muster. "Sure, Amber, what's up?"

"What were you doing upstairs in Ben's office?"

"Just seeing what his office looked like."

"You have no business snooping around in people's offices."

"I just wanted to see it."

Amber scowled. "You'd better come clean, 'cause you're in trouble."

Sweat trickled down the side of Aiden's jaw. He couldn't lose this job. "I wanted to find out Ben's last name. I thought it might be on his desk somewhere."

Amber looked over her shoulder and lowered her voice. "But why? Why did you want to know?"

Surprised by Amber's reaction, Aiden groped for an answer. "Well, uh, you always just say Ben, and I wondered what his last name was."

"And you didn't think to ask me?" She crossed her arms, her expression turning to frustration. "Look, I'm trying to help you. Ben told me he caught you. Now what's going on? Did you find out his name?"

Aiden envisioned his father waiting for him to return from work to cook supper and talk about his day. "Yes. I saw it on an envelope— Benjamin Bannister. I didn't take anything. I just saw the name and left." Amber flinched at the mention of Ben's last name. Aiden sighed. "I was curious, that's all."

"Does this have anything to do with the Mustang that lost its wheel? You told me Jordan was following you. Did he ask you for Ben's last name?"

"No, Jordan didn't ask for it. Is it a secret or something?"

"Never mind. Who wanted to know his name?"

Aiden couldn't get Vikki involved in this. "No one."

Amber shifted her hands to her waist. "I know Jordan's behind this, but you stay out of it. I'll figure out something to tell Ben."

Aiden and Amber jumped at the deep voice from behind. "My last name's not a secret, but there is a reason I'm keeping it quiet."

Amber spoke the question on Aiden's mind. "How long have you been there?"

"Long enough to know I have some explaining to do. Randy's got the counter, so let's talk a bit." Ben led them to a bench in the waiting area, which sat empty this late in the afternoon. "I want to talk in here, since I'd rather my son not see us."

Amber looked puzzled. "Is Aaron upstairs? I didn't know he came in today."

"He needed to get some paperwork done, so he came in through the back door a few minutes ago. He likes to work in the evening when there are no distractions."

Mr. Bannister's face relaxed. "You see, Aiden, my son ran into legal problems and spent some time in jail. I bought this business as an investment and hired Aaron to do our accounting and take care of any procedural necessities. It's a chance for him to start over." He cleared his throat. "People in Claymon, especially in the church he used to attend, know about his situation. So he wants to lay low for now. That's why we asked Amber not to broadcast our last name. In a town this size, people would make connections." He fixed his eyes on Aiden. "You know it now though, and I assume you've told someone. Why did you want to know?"

Aiden's mind scrambled to come up with a decent answer, but none appeared. "Um, I don't know."

Ben lowered his eyes at Amber, then looked directly at Aiden. "Do you like your job here?"

Aiden's voice trembled. "Yes, sir. I need it."

Ben rose from his seat. "Amber and Randy speak highly of your work, and they've told me how you help support your father. See that you stay downstairs and out of anyone's office."

Aiden let out a sigh of relief. "Yes, sir. Thank you."

Ben held his eyes briefly, then he nodded and walked toward the staircase. Amber headed to the counter.

Aiden sat for a moment, waiting for his heart to stop pounding, and whispered a prayer of thanks to the heavens. Amber locked the shop door and tended to end-of-the-day procedures on the computer.

He walked to her desk and said an awkward thank you.

"Don't worry about it, Aiden. Go finish your work."

As Aiden walked to the next car on his list, he spotted movement at the top of the stairs. Ben Banister's son stood at the rail with a stony stare fixed on him.

* * *

Lee slammed his fist on the desk after his father's footsteps faded down the hall. His act of revenge had spiraled out of control, and he could guess who asked Aiden to find out his dad's last name. Using his middle name couldn't save him now. It wouldn't take long for Vikki and her friends to put the pieces together.

Lee buried his head in his hands. He had to keep himself together. Vikki had the jacket. So what? That didn't link him to the crime, even if they found out who he was. Other people in town wore the same jacket. Nothing should tie the one Aiden found to him. He squeezed his eyes shut, picturing the meeting of Aiden and Vikki at the park. Aiden had handed her the jacket and the notes he'd found on his car and front door. But there was something else— some silver object Aiden passed to Vikki. Lee caught his breath, and panic twisted his mouth. The keychain with his initials! Terror seized him, pulsating through his temples. He paced the perimeter of his office. How had he forgotten about the keychain in his pocket?

What a fool he'd been to use that old jacket to wrap the lug wrench in, but who would have thought Aiden would find it shoved under some old oil pans in the back dumpster? He must have poked around, trying to fit in more trash, and unearthed the jacket.

Now that it was apparent someone had tampered with Jessie's car, Lee needed to point the evidence away from himself. Several minutes passed as he sat at his desk with his hands stretching the skin on his temples, planning his next move. A chilling laugh erupted from his mouth. No scrawny kid and conniving busybody could bring him down.

Lee crept back to the railing at the top of the stairs and spotted Aiden putting up his tools. No one stood at the counter, so he had a clear path. Lee hugged the left stair rail, then quietly slipped past the counter and out the front door. Scanning the lot, he spotted Aiden's old Malibu. Amber's car was the only other one left in the lot, and Lee knew she would exit the shop soon after Aiden. He dashed to his Lexus, drove it behind Aiden's vehicle, and slumped in his seat. After a few minutes, Aiden opened the shop door and headed for his car. Lee waited until Aiden put his hand on the door and then made his move.

"Wait! I need to talk to you."

Aiden yanked the handle, but Lee grabbed him before he could open his door. "Listen to me, kid. I'm trying to help you."

Aiden wrestled his arm loose. "Let go of me!"

Lee caught Aiden's arm again. "It's about Vikki and the red jacket you found."

He stopped cold. "How do you know about that?"

Lee freed Aiden's arm. "That's what I need to talk to you about. But not here. Somewhere we won't be seen by Amber."

"I'm not going anywhere with you."

Lee ground his teeth and glanced at the shop door. Amber would come out at any moment. Afraid Aiden might bolt, he forced an expression of concern he hoped seemed genuine. "Aiden, I'm trying to protect you. You're being lied to. Listen, meet me at McDonald's. We can talk there. Trust me."

Aiden's brow scrunched as if he were considering Lee's request. "Alright, I'll go."

Lee followed Aiden's car to McDonald's, inhaling deep breaths as he drove. He must play out the next moments carefully. He walked to a booth in the back of the restaurant, where Aiden sat with one leg on the outside of the booth.

"I'm here. What do you want?"

Lee smiled as if they were old friends. "A milkshake sounds good to me. I'll get you one, too."

"I don't want one."

"I'm ordering two shakes. Do you like chocolate?"

"I guess."

"Here, these look good, don't they?" Lee said, returning from the counter and setting a milkshake in front of Aiden. Lee raised his cup and took a sip of the sweet coldness. "Mmm. I love a good milkshake." He stared at his silent booth mate. "I need to fill you in on a few things, son. You seem like a good kid, and you deserve the truth. First of all, Randy's the one responsible for Jessie's accident."

Aiden's lips parted. "What do you mean? Randy told me he tightened the lug nuts."

"He did tighten them. But then a few days later, I overheard a conversation between him and Amber. He knows Jessie intimately, if you know what I mean."

"What?"

"An affair, Aiden. They had a fling, a one-night stand, and then she had the gall to call Randy's wife. No one would blame a man seeking revenge for that sort of betrayal." Lee's skin tingled with the irony of his words. "But Randy went too far."

"No way! Randy's old enough to be Jessie's father! I don't believe you."

"It's true, Aiden. I have no reason to lie to you."

Aiden shot him a look filled with skepticism. "Even if they did hook up, that doesn't prove anything."

"Yes, but Randy has the code to turn off the security cameras." Lee's gaze turned frosty. "Believe me, Aiden. I have ways of finding things out. Randy deliberately loosened the lug nuts on Jessie's car after switching off the surveillance cameras. Then, for another layer of security, he painted the camera lens pointed toward Jessie's car. And Amber's in on all of it. She helped him set the whole thing up."

"Why would she do that?"

"Randy's blackmailing her because he knows she is

stealing money from the shop. They're both shady characters."

Aiden lifted his chin. "How do I know you're telling the truth? Does your father know this?"

"Of course not, and he doesn't need to know. However, there is a big problem. The jacket Randy used to wrap up the lug wrench he used to loosen Jessie's wheel belonged to me."

Aiden gawked at him. "How would Randy get your jacket?"

"I carried it in my car for months, and when I got a job here I brought it in the shop one day just to have around as an extra. Somehow it ended up in the lost items box, and I just left it there. Randy must have grabbed it to wrap his lug wrench in then hid it in the dumpster where you found it. I assume he didn't know the jacket was mine. But who knows, maybe he did. He needed a scapegoat after all."

Aiden massaged his forehead. "Why are you telling me all this?"

"Because I know you found the jacket in the dumpster, Aiden. I hope you haven't thrown it away." He smiled at the shock on Aiden's face. "I just need you to give it back to me."

Aiden's hands shook, and he swallowed. "Why would I take it? It's— it's probably still in the dumpster."

Lee clenched his teeth. "I left a keychain with my initials in a pocket, and I can't have Vikki showing it around." He flinched at his slip of the tongue, desperation threatening his composure. "I need that jacket. I won't take the fall for this!"

Aiden's face twisted. "How do you know Vikki has the jacket?" His jaw dropped, and a bead of sweat ran down the side of his nose. "You trailed me the night I found the jacket and followed me to the park. You wrote the notes!"

Lee's jaw twitched, and he flexed his fists balled up under the table. "I need you to get the jacket," he said with clipped words. "I'll make sure Randy pays for his crime, and if you don't give it to me, I'll take you down with him."

"You followed me. You know I gave the jacket to Vikki."

Lee's eyes narrowed into long slits. "That's right, and I can either protect you or make you wish you'd never gone near that dumpster."

Aiden's voice quivered. "But how do I get it back?"

Lee pressed his hands against the table, leaned forward, and spoke with a threatening tone. "I don't know. Tell Vikki that Randy caused Jessie's wreck. Or tell her Amber wants to turn the jacket over to the police. I don't care. Just get it!" His eyes bulged with frustration. "Bring it to the shop tomorrow morning before the store opens. We'll burn the jacket in the barrel out back."

Aiden stuttered. "I'll— I'll try."

Lee reached over the table and grabbed Aiden's hoodie by the neck. "You'll do better than try. Bring the jacket to me. Call Vikki if you want. Tell her the police are demanding you return the jacket. Have it at the shop tomorrow morning by 6:30." He dropped his hands from Aiden's collar, and his lips curled in a dark smirk. "Oh, and don't tell Amber I told you this. Like I said, she's protecting Randy." With a dark scowl, Lee stalked off.

* * *

Aiden stared at his runny milkshake, dread chaining him to his seat. He needed to get to his car. To go somewhere and think. After several minutes, he headed out the door, scanning the parking lot in case Lee lurked nearby. He drove aimlessly around town, keenly aware of every vehicle behind him.

Aiden's head throbbed, conflicting thoughts jarring his brain. One thing was sure; Lee was lying about Randy and Amber. Or was he? Maybe Vikki was the liar. Aiden thought of the kindness in her eyes the morning she'd found him after his night in the park. No, he trusted her.

That's why he'd met her at the park the second time to show her the red jacket. But Lee's anger scared him. Could he be telling the truth? This crazy mess began when he'd left a job unfinished the night his father fell. Aiden glanced at the clock on the dashboard and took the next road that led home. Was everyone lying to him? After he fixed dinner for his father, he would place a call to Vikki and hope she wouldn't betray him.

CHAPTER SEVENTEEN

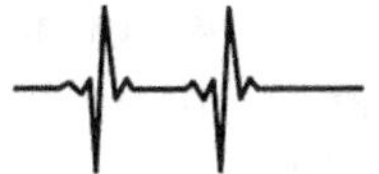

Jessie was a somber passenger as Jordan drove back to the rehabilitation hospital. "Are you okay, Love?" he asked.

"I'm not sure," Jessie said. "I'm emotionally drained." The bundle with the jacket and lug wrench lay across her lap. She wondered why she felt the need to hold it. "When will you turn this in?"

"Tomorrow. I'm going to get a hold of Officer Trent in the morning and see if he'll stop by the station." Jordan gave her a sideways glance. "It's for the best, don't you think? The police need to be brought into this mess."

"Yes, but we don't know who's in danger now." Jessie was confident about one thing; Lee had loosened her lug nuts as revenge. The man was a treacherous psychopath pinning the blame on Randy to cover up his activities. When Aiden had called Vikki earlier, she convinced him that Lee was lying. The problem was keeping Lee from further action until the police could intervene. "Do you think Aiden's safe?"

Jordan parked near the hospital door. "I think so as long as Aiden pretends he's cooperating with Lee. My guess is that Lee plans to destroy the jacket or figure out some way to link it to Randy."

"The man's a lunatic! Why not take the jacket to the police station right now?"

"I think it's better to let Lee believe Aiden is trying to get the jacket for him, at least for now. Besides, I want to talk to Trent first, and I don't know if he's on duty tonight." Jordan wiped Jessie's tears with his finger. "It's okay to be angry, Love. Just don't ever let it control you." He tapped the tip of her nose. "We can't let you get any anger wrinkles, now, can we?"

Jessie wiped her hot cheeks. "It may be too late for that."

"Let's get you back to your room. I'll talk them into letting me stay a little bit." Jordan reached over, grabbed a tube-shaped object from the glove compartment, and shoved it in his pocket.

"What's that?"

"I'll show you when we get inside. Come on."

Jordan snapped the wheels back on her chair, positioning it for Jessie to transfer. He helped her get seated and walked beside her to the hospital door. Jordan flashed a smile and winked at the receptionist. She didn't mention visiting hours.

* * *

Lee pulled Diane inside the door and seized her in a hard kiss, his hands pressing against her waist. "What did you tell Patrick you were doing?"

Diane pulled away, color sweeping the side of her

face. "This is my Bible study night. I told him I was eating dinner with a friend first."

Lee smirked. "So, I'll order pizza."

"What do you want, Lee? I'm going to my group. You said you needed to see me."

"A Bible study? Still trying to be a good girl?"

"Vikki attends our group. I've got a rumor brewing about her trying to steal the benefit money," Diane said, ignoring Lee's sarcasm. "Oh, I have it in cash like you wanted — three thousand dollars." She thrust it at him.

Lee snatched the money and waved it in the air. "Nice work. But how did you manage? You told me Brandon took the envelope."

"He did, and Patrick picked it up at the church, but I offered to deposit the money for him since he was so busy."

"And you covered it?"

Diane threw him a peevish look. "Come on. I remember the tricks of the trade. It hasn't been that long since we worked our little scheme with the church offering."

Lee's eyes glinted. "It's called embezzlement, my dear. And it was a great sideline for a while."

She flung the empty envelope on a chair. "You have the money. I'm out after this. It should take care of the rest of my gambling debt."

Lee snorted. So naive of her to think he would let her go that easily. "Darling, you can't get out quite yet."

Diane glared at him. "You said this money would take care of what you owe your lawyer friends to help me."

One side of Lee's mouth rose in a sneering smile. "Are you forgetting I paid to terminate your pregnancy — a secret I'm guessing you don't want to be known."

Diane looked as if her worst nightmare had jolted her from sleep. "No, Lee. Please. You'll ruin me."

"Calm down. I can't afford a scandal any more than you can, but I need your help to make people believe Vikki's a thief before I let you off the hook."

"That's what I'm doing. I told you I'd planted seeds of suspicion. Just like I cast doubt on Jessie's character. What else do you want from me?" Bitterness colored her voice. "Don't you think we're about even? You bought my silence for your little act of revenge."

Lee stiffened as he fought to control his seething rage. He grabbed her shoulders and brought her face close. Her jaw quivered beneath his fingers. "Don't forget I know your secrets." The defiance in Diane's eyes infuriated yet intoxicated him. She didn't tame as easily as most women. Relaxing his grip, he caressed her arms. A little flattery went a long way with her type. "Diane, you make me crazy. You're beautiful and dangerous, just what I desire in a woman." He lifted her chin and crushed his lips against hers. "We were so good together. You need a real man like me."

Diane twisted out of his embrace. "I'm leaving now. You don't have to worry about me squealing. Like you said, we both have secrets." With fire in her eyes, she stormed out the door.

Lee collapsed into his recliner and picked up the bottle he'd left on the floor from the night before. How had he let his life spin out of control a second time? Coming back to Claymon was a colossal mistake, but his father's offer to help him make a new start had made sense. He'd planned to lay low, work hard, and be reinstated as a lawyer someday. Bringing the bottle to his lips, he breathed a mirthless laugh. He'd blown it all in an impulsive act of revenge.

And to make matters worse, he was entangled in Diane's mess. He regretted that drunken night when he'd taken Diane to bed and bragged about how he'd avenged Jessie's betrayal. It had shocked Diane, and he'd been a little fearful that she'd divulge his secret out of some remnant of the tattered morality she professed. But no, she needed him to help square away her gambling debt.

And her stupidity in getting pregnant worked in his favor. Paying for her abortion merely tightened his realm of control. She would do anything to keep that dirty little secret tucked away. It wasn't the first time he'd bought a woman's silence.

Lee wobbled on his feet as he walked to the refrigerator, where he grabbed a couple of slices of cheese, some deli ham, and a bottle of soda to ease his queasy stomach. He sat at the table, attempting to clear his mind. Aiden was scared, Lee was sure of that. But would he come through with the jacket? He'd likely contacted Vikki by now. Would they meet tonight?

Lee took his last gulp of soda. With food in his stomach, he felt good enough to head to the community park in case Aiden had asked Vikki to meet there like he did before. If he could get the jacket tonight, all the better. Lee sighed. It was worth taking a chance.

* * *

After excusing herself from Bible study early, Vikki fumbled with her keys as she unlocked the door to the church offices and debated whether to flip on the lights. It wouldn't be unusual for her to be in the office area. Yet, she didn't want to have to explain herself if someone should come by. Finally, she decided to leave the lights off hoping no one would notice her since the group met at the other end of the building. Walking quickly, she went down the hall and opened the conference door.

"Please, God, don't let me get caught," she prayed, touching the cross on her necklace, then pulled Patrick's jacket from its hanger and stuffed it under her Bible in the bag she carried. She locked the office, crept to the main door, and took off for Jeremy's new truck. Luckily, he hadn't found it strange when she said she wanted to drive it tonight. If Lee happened to come to the park, he would be looking for her car instead of a truck, and Aiden planned on taking his father's car.

Taking caution not to be seen, Vikki waited until turning out of the church lot before switching on her lights and heading to the park. She drove to a spot under a tree several feet from the trail entrance, glanced at the yellow and red clouds low in the western sky, then whispered a prayer for safety. Stepping gingerly on the dim trail as it meandered along the creek, she rounded the bend. She sighed in relief as Aiden came into view, sitting with his back against the tree. "Good, you're here." She held up her bag. "I've got the jacket."

Aiden stood and shook his head. "Here's the paint, but this is crazy, man."

"I know. Jeremy would flip out if he knew what we were doing. But it might buy Jordan some time to talk to Officer Trent. And if you don't produce a jacket tomorrow morning, Lee might harm you." Vikki held up the sleeve. "I still have the picture of Lee's jacket. We'll do the best we can to make our paint job look like the stain on his. Then you can take it to Lee tomorrow, like he said."

"Do you think he'll believe it's his?"

"He should. I think it's the same size, and I doubt he took time to notice a whole lot about the stain. Just pray he doesn't look for the keychain."

"How did you get away?"

Vikki felt her cheeks warm. "I'm supposed to be at Bible study."

"Whoa! You're looking for trouble."

Aiden laid the jacket on the ground, peered at the picture on Vikki's phone, and shook the can vigorously.

"Wait, Aiden. It might look more real if I put it on. It would be a better simulation."

"Yeah, you're right. Good idea."

Vikki zipped the jacket and stretched out her arm. "Try not to get paint on me. I'd have a hard time explaining that."

Aiden shook the can again and gave Vikki a hesitant look. "This is it." Black mist floated in the air and pooled on the jacket sleeve until Aiden righted the can. "Cool, it worked. But if anyone's around, they'll think we're up to something."

Vikki held her arm away from her nose until the paint thickened slightly, then carefully unzipped the jacket. "That'd be great. I can see the headline. Minister's Wife Caught Huffing Paint with Kid from Youth Group."

Aiden offered her a wry grin. "Like I said, you're looking for trouble." He helped ease her arm out of the sleeve. "The paint should dry to touch in about 30 minutes."

"It will be dark before long," Vikki said, "but let's wait a few minutes anyway." She laid the jacket on the ground. "Not bad. It looks almost like the paint stain on

Lee's jacket. It has a small tear in the neck where I ripped off the tag with Patrick's name on it, but if we fold it up like you found it, Lee might be fooled."

Vikki wrapped the jacket around the collapsible lug wrench Aiden had brought from the shop. She drew her hand to her mouth at a snapping sound. "Shh! Someone's coming." She nudged the paint can under some brush as Lee burst through the trees.

"My, my, Vikki, it's been a while, hasn't it? I must say I'm surprised you handed it over to Aiden so quickly." He grabbed the bundle and clutched it to his chest. "Now I've got the jacket, you morons. You have nothing on me."

"Just take it and leave us alone."

"Not so quick. I need some assurance this kid doesn't squeal."

"Why would I?" Aiden said, "You said Randy was the guilty one."

Lee threw the jacket down and shook Aiden's shoulders. "Yeah, and here's something to make sure you don't forget that," he shouted, cuffing Aiden's head. Hooking him behind the knees, Lee sent Aiden crashing to the ground.

Haunting images of Lee striking his wife overcame the fear that had paralyzed Vikki until this moment. The lug wrench had fallen from the jacket and lay within her reach. She grabbed it and lunged for Lee. Twisting around, he dodged a blow to his head, causing the wrench to bash into his shoulder. He howled with pain, cursed, and dove toward Vikki. The force of his hand across her cheek brought tears to her eyes.

Aiden regained his footing and picked up the wrench which had fallen from Vikki's hands. He rushed at Lee, ramming the tool into his gut. Lee clutched the site of the blow, letting Vikki tumble to the ground. She grabbed his foot and yanked it with all her strength. He lost his balance and fell to his knees. Fury streaming from his face, Lee crawled over to Vikki and landed a punch to her stomach. He staggered to his feet and kicked her until she rolled close to the creek's edge. Pain radiated through her abdomen and up her spine.

"Stop! She's pregnant!" Aiden yelled and rushed to Vikki's crumpled form.

Lee staggered to his feet and hauled Aiden up with him. Sweat dripped from his face.

"Neither of you saw me here, understand? Some random person attacked you." Pulling Aiden close, he said, "Remember, Randy's the one who loosened Jessie's wheel if anyone asks you. Don't forget, I know where your father lives, and I wouldn't want to have to hurt a helpless man."

"Don't you dare touch my father!"

Lee slammed Aiden below his chest. "Then keep your mouth shut."

Aiden bowed over, gasped, and sank to the ground.

Lee seized the jacket and rolled the lug wrench inside. He sneered at Vikki, who lay frozen with terror. "And I know you got caught trying to steal the benefit money, so don't be cute and tell Jeremy about this little meeting. I can ruin him, and his pathetic 'walk the talk' ministry." He limped down the trail, holding his side with one hand and clutching the jacket in his other. "I'll destroy everyone you care about if either of you talk," he shouted, his words fading behind him. Vikki closed her eyes, praying he wouldn't turn back.

"Vikki!" Aiden's voice cut through her haze. She

blinked in the darkness, then opened her eyes, remembering where she was. She put weight on her arms, groaning as she lifted herself to a sitting position. She licked a salty taste from her mouth. "I'm bleeding."

"You have a cut on your lip. It doesn't look bad, though. Can you stand?"

"I think so. It's mainly my stomach and side."

"Do you think the baby's okay?"

A wave of dread assaulted Vikki. "A fall can cause a miscarriage. I'm sure a punch to the stomach would be dangerous, too." She blinked back her tears. "How do you know I'm pregnant?"

"I heard from some kids at church. Things like that get around."

"It's dark. We need to get out of here."

"Can you walk? Maybe we should call Jeremy."

Vikki scolded herself and touched her midsection as she thought of Jeremy's reaction if he learned of her exploits. What if her actions caused her to lose their baby? "Let me try to walk to the truck and then see how I feel about driving."

"I don't know, Vikki."

"Help me up."

"Okay, I'll try."

Vikki cringed as Aiden heaved himself to a standing position, holding his gut. His earlier assessment rang true. It had been a crazy idea. With Aiden's help, she managed to rise to her feet. "Ooh, that hurts."

Clutching Aiden's arm, they hobbled to the tree, each footfall sending spasms of pain through her body. She leaned against the tree fighting the urge to slide down its trunk. Getting to the truck was imperative, but she couldn't find the strength to move. Every breath shook her with agony.

Aiden's jaw stiffened. "Give me your phone, I'm calling Jeremy. Or tell me his number."

With no energy left to protest, Vikki pointed to her book bag and let herself slip to the ground.

CHAPTER EIGHTEEN

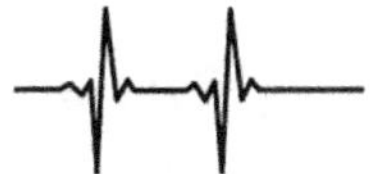

Jeremy glanced at the microwave clock as he led Heather to the couch for her bedtime stories that he'd delayed as long as possible. Vikki must be visiting with the girls after Bible study. Maybe they went out for a soda, though it was unlike her not to call. Or the group might be praying for someone. "Go ahead and pick three books, Heather. We'll be all ready for Mommy when she gets home."

Halfway through the second story, Jeremy's phone rang from where he had left it on the kitchen counter. He let it go to voicemail until he finished. "Daddy's going to check his phone. Stay right there and get the next book ready for me."

He tapped the voice mail from Vikki and was surprised at the male voice. "Jeremy, this is Aiden. Please call." Jeremy pressed the phone icon, and Aiden answered immediately. "Jeremy, Vikki's hurt. We're at the park and need you to come. Don't call anyone. Come alone."

"The park? Why are you— What happened? Is she hurt badly?"

"I'm not sure. We tried walking to the truck, but she couldn't make it."

"Hold on. I'll have to bring Heather, so it will take a minute. Is she bleeding?"

"Only a little from a cut on her lip. I, um, think she's hurt in the stomach."

Jeremy's blood chilled to the marrow. "I'll be there as soon as I can."

"Please come alone."

"Why? Wait! Can I talk to her?" But Aiden had disconnected.

After making a phone call to his parents, Jeremy spoke as casually as he could to Heather. "I have to go get Mommy. She hurt herself at the park."

The little girl put her hands on her hips. "It's dark outside. Mommy shouldn't be at the park."

"Yeah, you'd think that, wouldn't you?" Jeremy murmured.

"But who will take care of me?"

Jeremy ruffled his little daughter's hair. "You're coming with me, angel. Can you be a big girl and do what Daddy says? Gran and Gramps are meeting us at the park, so I can hurry to find Mommy."

Heather nodded and pranced to the couch. "Bun Bun is coming too," she said, holding the well-loved rabbit by its ear.

Jeremy gathered Heather, Bun Bun, and a blanket, then headed for the car. On the way out, he grabbed his medical kit. "I guess it's good she took the truck since your seat is in the car."

As he drove, he called Vikki's phone, and Aiden answered. "Where exactly are you?" Jeremy asked.

Aiden's directions told him what he needed to know. "Okay, hold on."

Jeremy pulled into the park. Hopefully, his parents were on their way. Their vehicle arrived a few seconds later. "Here they are, Heather, let's get you out."

Marianne hopped out of the car. "What's going on, Jeremy? Where's Vikki?"

"Vikki just had a little fall and I'm going to go get her."

"But why is she— "

Jeremy caught his mother's eye and angled his head toward Heather.

"Oh." She looked at her granddaughter. "Come home with Gran, Heather. We can read stories and have some cookies."

Heather's mouth drooped, and she clung to Jeremy's hand. "I want to go get Mommy."

Jeremy knelt level with Heather's eyes and lifted her chin. "Listen, Heather. I need you to do what I say," he said with a slight quiver. "It is too dark for little girls to walk in the woods, so I need you to go with Gran and Gramps."

"I want to go get Mommy."

"I know you do, but I need you to be brave and do what I say. I'll call Gran as soon as I get her all fixed up." He wiped a tear from her eye. "Can you do that for me? And say a little prayer for Mommy?"

Heather frowned but let Frank put her in the car seat he had moved to his vehicle. "Come on, Snicklefritz, I want some cookies, too."

Jeremy hugged Heather and thanked his parents. "I'll keep you informed." They nodded, and he hurried to the trail. Toting his first aid kit, he stepped over sticks and rocks, shining his flashlight directly on the path and walking as quickly as he dared. Rounding the corner, he found the two victims sprawled under the tree.

Aiden waved. "Over here, Jeremy."

Jeremy ran over and knelt in front of Vikki, wincing at her scratched face and the dull green color of her eyes. "Hey, baby. Where does it hurt?"

"My side mostly. It hurts when I breathe."

When he felt around her ribcage, she flinched and cried out. "I think you may have a cracked rib or two," Jeremy said.

Vikki's eyes filled. "What about the baby?"

Jeremy brushed his hand across his forehead. "You're still in the first trimester, so I'm not too concerned about injuries to the baby. We'll get you checked, though."

He looked at Aiden. "Are you okay? What happened here?"

"I'm not hurt bad. I think I'll have some bruises, though. Aaron, or Lee, I mean, got in a few gut punches."

Jeremy shifted incredulous eyes to Vikki. "Lee!" Vikki nodded, her eyes huge.

Forcing his attention back to Aiden, Jeremy carefully palpitated the teen's abdominal area finding no signs of organ injury. "I think you'll be sore for a few days, but I don't feel anything serious."

Jeremy sat on the ground and gazed at Vikki. "What the heck are you doing here?"

Vikki's voice was barely audible, "I brought Patrick's jacket to Aiden so he could give it to Lee."

"What? You lured him here!"

"No," Vikki held her side and grimaced, "Aiden was— ooh, ow!"

"Lee threatened me, Jeremy," Aiden said. "He knew Vikki had his jacket because he followed me after I found it and saw me give it to her. He told me to bring it to him tomorrow morning." He paused and looked at Vikki. "We decided to take Patrick's jacket to him instead."

Vikki groaned and raised a bit. "It's my fault, Jeremy. I thought if we painted a black stain on Patrick's jacket, Lee might think it was his own. He walked in on us, though."

Jeremy's head reeled. "I'll kill him." He stooped beside Vikki and tried to calm his trembling voice. "But why would you give him Patrick's jacket?"

Tears trickled down Vikki's face. "I thought he might be fooled, at least for a while, and it would give Jordan more time to get Lee's jacket to the police. That way Aiden would have a jacket to give Lee like he demanded." She wiped her eyes. "Lee did take it with him."

"This was your idea?" he said, teetering between anger and astonishment. "I can't believe you guys tried such a crazy trick. It's insane. Do you think Lee will fall for it?"

Aiden spoke up. "The paint wasn't completely dry, but he might not notice in a rush to get rid of the jacket."

Vikki pushed herself up a little more. "Hopefully, he won't remember the keychain he left in his pocket."

Jeremy shook his head. "I don't understand. If he believed you gave him his jacket, why did he beat you up?"

"To intimidate us." Vikki raised her chin. "But we fought back."

Jeremy read the defiance in her eyes and pushed back a smile, "I'm sure you did." He looked at the battered conspirators in wonder. "Let's get you out of here."

Vikki struggled to stand. "Okay, but I'll have to lean on you."

"No way. I'm calling for an ambulance."

Aiden grabbed Jeremy's arm. "No! Lee said not to tell anyone. He might be watching, and he'll hurt my father!"

"I can't carry Vikki without the risk of further injuries." Jeremy pushed back his bangs. "I guess I could call Jordan. He can pick up a carrier and come help."

"But Lee might see him!"

"Listen, Aiden, we have to get medical help. If Lee's still around, he already knows I'm here. He'll expect that I'll call for assistance. I'll make sure there's no ambulance or police." Jeremy angled his head. "If he's that close he's heard everything you guys told me."

"Jeremy's right," Vikki said. "Besides, Lee stormed off in a hurry. I'm sure he's gone."

After Jeremy called Jordan, the three sat beneath the tree with Vikki resting her head on Jeremy's shoulder and Aiden close on his other side. Jeremy let out a long breath. "All I can say is, you two are in big trouble." Vikki looked up at him with her huge green eyes. "Stop it," he said with the sternest look he could muster.

The sound of footsteps brought Jeremy to his feet. "Over here, Jordan."

"What are their injuries, Jeremy?" Jordan said, sizing up the scene.

"Aiden's bruised up, but I think he can walk."

"I can make it," Aiden said. "Just help Vikki."

"Vikki may have bruised or cracked ribs. That's why I didn't carry her out or help her walk."

"That's the right call."

Jordan's eyes moved from Adien to Vikki. "Looks like a wild party," he said with a playful tip of his mouth. "Come on, Preacher, let's haul them out of here."

Aiden limped over to them. "I said I could walk."

Jeremy caught Jordan's closed-lipped grin. "I'm sure you can, buddy. Just yell if you need help."

Using the stretcher Jordan had carried along the trail, he and Jeremy transported Vikki to the parking lot with Aiden hobbling behind. Aiden insisted he could drive, and Jordan agreed as long as he followed Aiden home.

Jeremy filled Jordan in on the details of the evening. "Aiden's going to have to explain things to his father. Maybe you can help, Jordan."

"Yeah, we'll have to come up with something good," he said with a wink toward Aiden.

"How about the truth?"

Jordan lifted his eyebrows. "I think we'll have to come up with something better than that."

"Jordan, don't you— "

"Chill, Preacher Boy, I'll do the honorable thing."

Leaving the truck parked in the lot, Jeremy helped Vikki get in the car and headed for the emergency room. The doctor thought Vikki's ribs and chest muscles were deeply bruised instead of cracked. She was reluctant to order X Rays because of Vikki's pregnancy but suggested she have an MRI if her pain worsened.

The physician sent Vikki home with prescription strength pain medicine to use sparingly and instructions to modify her activities. She also suggested it might be more comfortable for Vikki to sleep in a recliner for a week or two. Jeremy called his parents with an update. Since Heather was asleep, Marianne offered to bring her home the next morning.

Jeremy snuck a sideways glance at Vikki on the drive home. She sat leaning toward the door with her head against the window. He sighed, relieved that her only injuries were a few scratches and a bruised rib cage, but her evening's endeavors unnerved him.

Vikki raised her head as the truck pulled into their tree-lined driveway. "Are you mad at me, Jeremy?"

Jeremy angled his head and gazed at her. "Let's just say it's a good thing I love you."

"You are mad."

"Why don't we get you settled before we talk?"

Jeremy helped Vikki inside and stayed close as she readied herself for the night. He brought pillows and blankets into the living room and fixed her a bed on the recliner. When she shuffled into the room, he helped her lower herself onto the couch and sat beside her.

"I'm sorry, Jeremy."

Jeremy caressed her hand. "I'm not angry exactly. More surprised, I guess. You've behaved way out of character the last few days. And done things I never would have expected."

"I know. But I needed to help Adien. He's afraid, and I never do anything brave. I'm always scared to act, but this time I felt like I had to. I thought maybe we could fool Lee."

"Well, you acted alright. Maybe you did trick Lee, at least for the moment. But Vikki, you put yourself and our baby in danger."

"We didn't think Lee would show up. And the only danger would have been in the morning if Lee figured out the jacket wasn't his. Aiden agreed he had to risk it. I guess it was a bad idea."

"Well, what's done is done. If nothing else, you've set things in motion. Aiden forced Lee's hand by finding the jacket. Then Lee incriminated himself by confronting you guys at the park." Jeremy said. He helped her to the recliner and covered her with a blanket.

She sighed and touched his cheek. "I love you, Jeremy."

"I love you, too." He carried his pillow and blanket to the couch.

"Are you going to sleep in here?"

"Yeah, I want to stay close at least for tonight."

"I'm sorry for causing all this trouble."

Any remnants of anger in Jeremy dissolved as he met the eyes of the woman God had blessed him with. He kissed her in the gentle way he knew she loved. "I'm sure you did what you thought best. Good night, little schemer."

* * *

Jessie's phone rang a few minutes after she'd transferred to her bed. "Hey, Love. I don't want to scare you, but keep the pepper spray handy, okay? I wouldn't think Lee would be stupid enough to try to harm you, but he may be desperate at this point."

Jessie's hand trembled as Jordan told her about Vikki's and Aiden's encounter with Lee.

"That's unbelievable, Jordan. Could the blows to her stomach hurt the baby?"

"Vikki's being checked out now. The baby's probably fine. She may have a couple painful cracked ribs to deal with, though."

"And Aiden?"

"Bruised and battered, but he'll mend. Jessie, did you know about this plan of theirs?"

"Absolutely, not. It sounds a little misguided."

"Ya think? But who knows? It might work if Lee ditches the jacket without realizing it isn't his. I've kept

Officer Trent in the loop. He's on patrol tonight and agreed to meet me."

They said their goodbyes, and Jessie leaned on her pillow, mulling over the past few days. A flicker of hope had been rekindled in her soul and grown into a flame, lighting up new possibilities. Difficulties lay ahead, but she could manage them. Lee Bannister, who was most likely plotting another act of revenge, worried her. But he'd be exposed tomorrow morning when Jordan delivered the jacket, lug wrench, and keychain to the police. Those items and Aiden's testimony would be enough evidence for an arrest.

At least, that's what Jordan said he believed. Even so, he'd left her some protection in case Lee somehow gained access to her room. She tucked the cylinder under a magazine on her bedside table. A smile spread across her face as she thought of living life with the man whose love and encouragement never failed her.

* * *

Still trying to figure out his next move, Lee dragged himself over each step to his office and dropped the bundle on his desk. Should he burn the jacket in the barrel behind the shop? He swiped at a dark spot on his hand. The wet smudge on his finger didn't smell like ink. Grabbing the jacket, he rubbed the stain and brought his fingers to his nose. Paint! But how could the paint be wet after all these weeks?

Lee unfolded the jacket and ran his thumb along the neckline. He didn't remember tearing the tag off his collar. Fingers of dread crawled up his neck. The keychain! Unzipping the top pocket, he felt around. It wasn't there. He checked the other pockets. Nothing.

Vikki had kept it, but why? Noticing a security pouch in the jacket's lining, he pulled out an old charge receipt. Bile rose in his throat as he read the signature— Patrick Johnson.

Profanities spewed from Lee's mouth, and prickles chilled the blood in his veins. He flung paperwork and his desk lamp to the floor with a furious swipe. Wild with rage, he tore at the jacket until a pocket ripped off. He crushed it into a ball and hurled it across the room. Seizing the lug wrench, he struck the wall, and a crack opened into a gaping hole. Lee staggered to his desk and collapsed into the chair, his shoulders heaving as he inhaled. He reached down to the bottom drawer of his desk and raised the bottle of vodka to his mouth. After two gulps, he propped his head and covered his eyes. They'd destroyed him. His jacket, keychain, and the lug wrench he used might already be in the hands of the police.

Lee stomped to the stairway and leaned over the top rail. Would a fall kill him or break his neck, leaving him an invalid? He snorted and backed away. A helluva sight that would be— wheelchair-bound in some nursing home playing bingo with Jessie.

The lawyer mentality Lee had perfected for years kicked in. His defeat wasn't inevitable. Vikki and Aiden's hoax had only been partially successful since he'd discovered the truth before getting rid of Patrick's jacket. All he needed was a plan, and he had a secret ace in the hole. He limped down the steps and tapped Diane's name on his phone screen as the shop door clicked behind him.

* * *

As Jordan disconnected his call to Jessie, he entered the school's parking lot to meet Michael Trent. He pulled his car beside the officer and powered down his window. "Thanks for meeting me, Michael."

"No problem." Trent took the bag from Jordan. "So, the lug wrench you think was used to loosen Jessie's wheels is in here?"

"Yes, along with Lee's jacket and keychain."

"Tell me what this is all about."

Jordan explained Vikki and Aiden's scheme, including how Lee had followed Aiden to the park and taken off with Patrick's jacket.

Trent raised his eyebrows. "Somebody's been watching too many crime shows."

"Do you think Lee's fingerprints will be liftable after so long? Other people may have used the wrench, too."

"Maybe. We may have enough evidence without prints, but I'll have them processed. Did you tell me that Lee's been arrested before?"

"Yes, last year. He spent a few months in jail for battery."

"Good. That will speed things up if prints are detected."

"And Randy can be fingerprinted if needed."

Officer Trent looked directly at Jordan. "I don't suppose you had anything to do with this little escapade of Aiden and Vikki's."

"Come on, Trent, even I couldn't come up with something that screwy," Jordan said with a grin. "But you gotta admit, it was gutsy."

"Hmm. What did Jeremy think about it?"

"Oh, Preacher Boy was fried alright, but it didn't last. Vikki just makes eyes at him and he melts. It's pathetic, man."

Trent laughed. "Well, let me get this over to the fingerprint lab. Finding Lee's prints on the wrench can't hurt, even if other prints are on it, too." He shifted his feet. "Remember, Jordan, this could take time. I can try pulling in some favors, but we're still talking a day or two. And even if Lee's prints are found, it's not proof he did anything. It just tells us that at some time Lee held the wrench."

"Can't you arrest him for roughing up Aiden and Vikki?"

Trent paused and hooked his fingers around his belt. "Not sure it would be the best idea to alert him that the police are involved." He held up the bag. "Let's see if we have anything here first. And like I said, we may not need prints if Lee makes a move first."

"But you aren't going to do anything yet?"

"I didn't say that. I might shake a few trees."

"Thanks again, Trent."

"No problem. And hey, let me handle this."

"What do you mean?" Jordan said with a look of innocence. "You think I'd interfere with you doing your job?"

* * *

Lee shuffled into his apartment, still waiting for a response from Diane. Just as he was about to text her again, his phone chimed. "It's Sunday night, Lee. Not easy to get away. I made an excuse that I needed something from the store. You can call now."

Lee immediately tapped Diane's number.

"What do you want?"

"I'm in trouble Diane. I'll explain later, but I may have to leave for a while if things get messy."

"So, what does that have to do with me?"

Lee chewed the sides of his mouth. He needed her to be his ally. "Diane, darling, I'm going to need some money since I won't be working for a while. But more importantly, I need you to do a little favor for me."

"How am I supposed to get you money? I'm not a bank."

"Come now, Diane, you know there's always a way. What about the missionary money that remains uncounted in that bucket in Patrick's office? We've looted that before."

"I know, but only small amounts at a time."

"So, a weekly fifty will be fine."

"I'm sick of this, Lee."

"I know, darling. Just a few more months, and we'll be able to run off together."

Diane's sigh was audible. "I told you before. I'm not about to leave Patrick."

Lee's frustration threatened to boil over. "Why not? He's weak, a loser who can't stand up against anyone. He let that self-righteous Jeremy take over the church."

Diane's silence rattled him, so he switched to his syrupy tone. "Come on, gorgeous. We'll talk all about how you deserve better later. Right now, I need you to do the favor I mentioned, and all your little secrets will stay safe with me."

"What is it, Lee? I'm not promising anything."

"I'll be able to erase all the rest of your gambling debts if you come through for me. And don't forget, you want to keep your virtuous reputation."

"Let's hear it."

"You're great at spreading rumors. This is just upping the ante a bit."

Lee outlined his plan and ended the call. He fell back

in his recliner with the satisfaction that he still possessed persuasive skills after years of law practice. Convincing Diane to agree had drained him, though. He reached for his whiskey bottle.

After a few drinks, Lee relaxed enough to contemplate his choices. Hiding out might not be the best idea after all—no need to draw attention to himself. Staying put would be better, at least for now. Diane's acting skills were sufficient to pull off his plan, and he would be there to corroborate her story. He could always make a quick getaway if needed, but he counted on Diane. She always came through.

CHAPTER NINETEEN

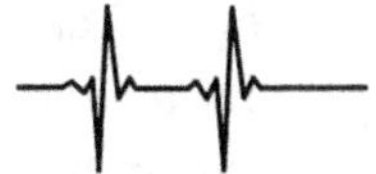

Jordan finished the last of his breakfast omelet and pushed away from the table. He grinned at his co-worker Rachelle. "Hey girl, how about taking my plate?"

"Ha! Right," she said as she shoved her plate toward him. "I believe you're on KP duty."

Jordan let out a playful sigh as he gathered the dishes. "Yeah, well. You can't blame a guy for trying."

Rachelle lifted her eyes to the ceiling. "How does Jessie put up with you?"

Jordan shrugged. "She won't wait on me either."

Jeremy looked at Jordan with teasing eyes. "Well, that's an understatement. Jessie's got you wrapped around her little finger."

Jordan clutched his chest. "Come on, Preacher Boy, you're killing me. I've got a reputation to keep here." Snickers rose from around the table, and Jordan tapped Jeremy's shoulder. "Like you're one to talk."

"By the way, how is Jessie?" Phil asked after the

laughter died down. "You mentioned she might be going home soon."

"Doing great. I'm hoping she'll be discharged this week."

As Jordan stood to go after the dish cart, his two-way radio sounded. "Lieutenant Raycom to the front desk."

"Be right there," he answered. "Phil, will you start the cleanup? I'll be back as soon as I can."

Phil nodded, and Jordan headed toward the lobby. As he approached the desk, he caught sight of Diane.

"What are you doing here?"

"I need to talk to you. And I need Jeremy to hear this, too."

Jordan turned away. "Don't have time."

"Wait," Diane said, taking hold of his arm. "It's about Jessie." She clasped her hands to her chest. "Please," she whispered. "I need to talk to both of you."

Something in Diane's expression told Jordan to listen. "I'll give you five minutes. I'm on duty." He called for Jeremy using his phone instead of the radio.

Jordan led Diane to his office and pointed to a table with three chairs around it. As soon as they sat down, Jeremy appeared at the door.

"What's this about?"

"Come in, Jeremy. Diane says she has information about Jessie we need to hear."

Jeremy took a seat and stared at Diane. "Well?"

Diane laid her phone on the table and began. "I have something to tell you that I heard from a source close to the situation. Lee didn't tamper with Jessie's car." She took a deep breath. "It was Randy."

Jordan's head jerked up, and he exchanged a glance with Jeremy. "Randy? What are you talking about? He tightened the lug nuts when Aiden got called away."

"I'm sure he told you that, and he may have. But he didn't tell you about his other deeds." Diane looked at Jordan with an expression he thought untypical of her usual self-assurance. "Randy loosened her lug nuts as a warning when…" Diane's voice held a slight tremor. "Jessie called his wife."

Jordan leaned forward with his elbows on the table. "What are you talking about? Why would Jessie call Randy's wife?"

"Because they had an affair, and Randy jilted her."

Jordan's hand landed hard on the table. "Get out!"

Jeremy eyed Jordan, then stepped toward Diane. "I don't know who fed you that line, but you need to leave."

Diane rose from the table and gave Jordan a meaningful glance. "Maybe Jessie isn't the angel you think she is. It wouldn't be the first time for her, would it?"

Jordan shot from his chair, tipping it over. He took a step toward her. "Get out," he said through gritted teeth.

"Okay, okay. I'm leaving. Just thought you'd want to know the truth."

"Diane," Jeremy said, planting his hand on Jordan's shoulder, "if this story's for real, tell us where you heard it."

"I can't tell you that. I told you what I know, and I'm leaving now." Diane walked to the door and pulled it open. She hesitated for a second, uncertainty etched on her features, then stepped back and closed the door. Putting a finger to her lips, she tapped her phone. "We were being recorded. I just turned the app off."

Absolute bewilderment twisted Jordan's face. "What?"

"All I just told you was a lie."

"What kind of game are you playing?" Jeremy demanded.

Diane cast a look toward the door. "It's not a game, and I've got to get out of here. He's waiting at the grocery down the road. I had to make the conversation sound real so he'll believe it when he listens."

"Who?" Jeremy asked.

"Lee." Diane's face contorted, and her eyes filled. "I couldn't go through with it. Lee's the guilty one," she said and walked through the door.

"Did he tell you that?" Jeremy started after her, but she kept walking. "You need to call the police if you have information like that."

"Let her go, Jeremy. We can't have a scene here." Jordan sank into a chair and motioned for his partner to do the same. "Sit down for a minute."

Jeremy sat in the chair across from Jordan and rubbed his forehead. "What now? I don't get it. Everyone at church knows about Lee's abuse of his wife, but what kind of connection would Diane have with Lee?"

"Who knows? And where does the truth lie in all this? Can we trust Diane?"

"We both know that Randy didn't loosen the lug nuts, and Jessie certainly didn't have an affair with him. It's the same story Lee told Aiden to spread around, so maybe she's legit. Should we contact Officer Trent?"

"I don't know. Let's see what Diane does. This could be some kind of bait for us to grab."

"But to what end? It doesn't make sense."

"I haven't a clue. By the way, how is Vikki?"

"Bruised ribs, instead of cracked, thankfully. She's sore, but okay."

Jordan shook his head. "That was some crazy plot. I wonder if Lee figured it out. Maybe that's why he sent

Diane here— some desperate ploy to turn attention away from him."

"Who knows what game he's playing? Maybe he's sending Diane with that story to everyone."

Though Jordan didn't believe the story Diane told about Jessie having an affair with Randy, hearing the words jolted him. He framed his face with his hands, jumbled thoughts playing havoc with his mind. "I don't know, but we've got to get back to work before someone comes looking for us."

"You look shell-shocked. I'll go help with the cleanup. Stay here as long as you need to. I'll check with you in a few minutes, and we'll decide what to do." Jeremy looked back before walking out the door. "Don't torment yourself, Jordan. You know Jessie's heart."

Jordan met his eyes and nodded. "Go on. I'll be alright. I'll text Jessie in a few minutes to give her a heads up that Diane might visit her."

Jordan held his head as thoughts and images he'd never allowed himself to entertain flooded his mind. He knew about the few years Jessie had strayed from her faith, and he'd told her truthfully it didn't matter to him. He loved her for the woman she was now. Still, imagining her in Lee's arms sent a wave of nausea over him. And somehow Diane knew Jessie's secrets. He'd seen it in her eyes.

Jordan rubbed his temples, attempting to force the images out of his mind, but other doubts surged. Would he be able to care for Jessie the way she deserved? Marianne's words echoed in his mind, "Your life will change drastically. Do you plan to help her with her catheter and bowel program?" He knew adjustments would be necessary. That wouldn't be a problem. Neither would their intimate relationship. He'd researched the topic of intimacy when dealing with paraplegia.

Jeremy's words the evening after dinner with Jessie's parents rattled Jordan the most. Was he trying to be a hero out of a misguided sense of duty? He dropped his head on folded arms and cried out in prayer. "God, help me be the husband Jessie needs. I can't do it without you. I need you to replace these doubts with courage." He prayed to the God he'd known since childhood until peace filled his soul. A shrill alarm brought him abruptly to his feet. "In Jesus' name, Amen," he said and raced out the door.

Jordan called on his ability to quickly change focus and concentrate on urgent tasks as he responded to the alarm. Jeremy caught up with him, and they headed for the emergency vehicles.

"You okay?"

Jordan nodded, appreciating the accountability his fellow first responders expected from each other. "I'm fine. Thanks for checking. I didn't get a text off to Jessie yet."

* * *

Lee held his side as he stepped out of his car. He walked up to Diane's vehicle and peered in her window. "How did Jordan react to our little story?" Diane handed Lee her phone, and he smirked as the conversation replayed.

"It's a crazy story Lee. I don't think Jordan believed me."

Lee slid into the passenger seat. "Maybe not, but you planted seeds of doubt. And with both of us telling the same story, it will at least cast suspicion on Randy."

"Randy will deny it, and so will Jessie. Remember, Jordan has your jacket and the lug wrench you used."

Lee's hands clenched, and he suppressed the urge to slap the insolence from her face. "I know that! I wore gloves, and a lot of fingerprints could be on that wrench, including Randy's. Randy could have easily gotten a hold of my jacket from the lost and found. As for Jessie, you're going to tell her the same story, only twist it and let on that Randy thought Jessie snubbed him so he wanted to teach her a lesson. You know, make it sound like Randy's mentally ill." Lee frowned at the wavering look in Diane's eyes. "What's wrong? You can't back out, now."

"You're the mental case, Lee. People aren't going to believe your lies."

Lee leaned over and grabbed her hair, yanking it until she cried out. His jaw muscles tightened, and his tongue burned. "Don't push me." Fighting for control, he released his grip at the sight of the horrified expression on Diane's face. "They'll believe, you'll see," he said with a condescending smile. "Go to the hospital this morning while Jordan and Jeremy are at work."

Diane rubbed the back of her head and wiped the tears from her eyes. "Alright, I'm going."

"You look awful," Lee said, pulling out his keys and billfold. He handed her a fifty and took a key off his chain. "Here's the key to my apartment. Buy some cosmetics and fix your face at my place. Pull yourself together before you visit Jessie. I want you to be somewhat believable. Just leave the key under the doormat. I have to get to work."

Diane grabbed the money but tossed the key in Lee's lap. "I'm not driving to your apartment. I'll get ready at home. Patrick's at work."

Lee chuckled. "Suit yourself, darling," he said and opened his door. "Don't forget to record your conversation with Jessie. Come over this evening so I can listen to it. I don't want to chance meeting you in public again today. I'm guessing Jordan may have gotten the police involved by now."

"Patrick and I have a group meeting tonight that I have to attend. I won't be able to meet you until tomorrow morning."

"Are you serious?" Lee swore and glared at her. "Be at my apartment by 6:30 in the morning then!"

Diane gave her head a toss. "I'll have to wait until Patrick leaves for work."

Lee grabbed her shoulders and pulled her face to his. "Listen to me! You get there as soon as possible." He slammed the door behind him.

Lee sat in his Lexus, gripping the steering wheel until Diane's car drove out of sight. Maybe he'd been too rough, but he couldn't afford her backing out now. With shaky hands, he reached for the bottle he'd purchased before Diane arrived. A few drinks of vodka would be undetectable on his breath, so it was a perfect choice if he needed it while working. A sip right now would calm his frazzled nerves.

* * *

Aiden limped into the shop, every step reminding him of the bruise trailing from his lower stomach to his thigh. He kept his head down as he passed the counter, but Randy let out a whistle. "Wow, kid, that must have been some kind of fight."

"Nah, just messing around with the guys."

"Messing around? That's a mean-looking lump on the side of your face."

Aiden's hand went to his cheek. "I, uh, I guess it got a little rough."

Amber looked up from her computer screen. "My gosh, Aiden, who did that to you?"

"I'm fine," Aiden said and hobbled to his workstation. He glanced at the staircase, wondering if Lee had come to work. Was he up there plotting his revenge, or would he lay low for a while and wait? Aiden agreed with Jordan and Jeremy that Lee's threat to hurt his father was a scare tactic to keep Aiden quiet because Lee couldn't afford any more trouble. Aiden didn't need a threat anyway. He wasn't saying a word.

The door jingled, and Aiden raised his head. Lee passed the front counter without speaking to Amber and headed for the staircase. His stride was off a bit, and he clutched his side as he climbed the stairs. Reaching the landing, Lee looked out over the shop. Aiden lowered his head, but not before he caught Lee's menacing glare. Aiden grabbed his tools and joined another mechanic to assist with a brake repair. Amber approached him as he finished replacing the caliper assembly on the car's last brake.

"When you finish that wheel, I need to talk to you."

Aiden's stomach flipped. "I'm almost done."

"I'll be in the conference room."

Aiden lifted the wheel and secured it. He spoke with the other mechanic and then left to meet Amber.

"Come in and have a seat, Aiden."

Amber averted her eyes as if she were hesitant to begin. Finally, she looked directly at Aiden. "A policeman came to the shop before it opened this morning so he could talk to me."

Aiden felt the color drain from his face. "Oh?"

"Listen, Aiden, remember when Jordan and Jessie's brother came by a few days ago with evidence that someone loosened her lug nuts. Apparently, someone turned off the security cameras the night before Jessie picked up her car."

"Really?"

"Have you heard anything else? Has Randy talked to you about it?"

Aiden shuffled his feet. "No."

"I couldn't believe an employee of mine would do such a thing, but now I don't know what to think."

"You don't think I did it, do you?"

"No. I think you know something, though. I've caught Aaron, I mean Lee, glaring at you more than once."

Aiden glanced in the direction of the staircase. "You think Lee did it?"

"I'm not sure, but I know about the jacket and keychain. I didn't let on the day Jordan and Jeremy visited, but the initials match Lee's—L.A.B.— Lee Aaron Bannister. The police officer questioned me about both Randy and Lee, though."

"What did you tell the police?"

"Everything I just told you."

"So why did you want to talk to me?"

Amber glanced at Aiden's swollen cheek. "Did you get into a tussle with Lee? I thought I saw him limping a bit this morning when he came in."

Aiden looked down. "Can I go now?"

Amber crossed her arms. "Yes. I just want you to know that I'm on your side. You need to tell me if Lee is threatening you in some way."

Aiden hesitated for a minute before he stood up. "Uh,

thanks." He left the conference room and wiped the sweat from his forehead, fighting an urge to look toward the staircase as he passed. Aiden started his next work order. He concentrated as best he could, keeping an eye on the stairs praying Lee wouldn't leave his office and come toward him waving Patrick's jacket like a wild man.

As the morning wore on, Aiden's hope that Lee believed the jacket was his and had disposed of it before coming to work seemed increasingly possible. By early afternoon, he was relaxed enough to take a break but skipped his plans to run to McDonald's and purchased a soda and chips from the vending machine in the lounge. As long as Lee was in the building, Aiden wasn't leaving.

After finishing his meager lunch, Aiden headed back to the garage. At the sound of footsteps, he moved behind a shelving unit. Looking straight ahead, Lee walked out the shop door. Aiden stepped out from behind the shelving and caught Amber's eye before she turned her attention to the customer at the service desk.

CHAPTER TWENTY

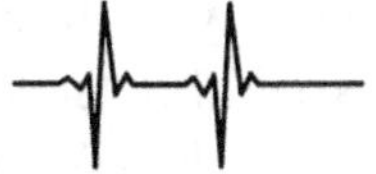

Lee's anxiety over the prospect of Diane bailing on him escalated. He drove to her affluent neighborhood. Diane's car wasn't in the driveway, and Patrick would be at work by now. Lee walked up the flower-lined sidewalk in case Diane's car was in the garage and rang the doorbell. To his relief, no one answered the door. At least Diane wasn't hiding out at home. She might already be at Hope Rehab with Jessie. He chuckled as he imagined the look on Jessie's face when Diane told her Randy loosened her lug nuts. Even if she doubted Diane's story at first, Aiden was also pointing the blame at Randy. At least he was if he knew what was good for him.

Diane and Patrick's sprawling two-story house with its manicured lawn rankled Lee. A few months ago, he'd lived in a prestigious neighborhood with his wife and young daughter instead of alone in a low-rent apartment complex.

But that was before two scheming women had taken everything from him. A pampered woman like Vikki couldn't understand how his wife, with her emotional problems, needed to be disciplined for her own good. And Jessie's naive belief that their one-night stand meant he loved her was ludicrous. Yet because of them, the court had slapped him with sanctions, and he barely escaped permanent disbarment, not to mention spending two months in jail.

Lee sat in the driveway, pondering his next move. Aiden had double crossed him, letting Vikki know about their talk at McDonald's. Did Vikki believe the story about Randy? Lee smacked his forehead. Of course, she didn't! What was wrong with him? Why else would Aiden and Vikki have tried to trick him with Patrick's jacket? It must be the booze messing with his head. His entire future depended on Diane's acting skills, and he had growing doubts about her loyalty. Lee pulled out of the driveway and took the road leading him to Hope Rehabilitation Hospital. He'd make sure Diane came through for him.

* * *

"Get some rest, Vikki, and take care of yourself. I can't believe that stunt you and Aiden pulled, but it may prove to be helpful."

"I don't know about that. Like I said, Jeremy wasn't exactly thrilled."

"Obviously, he wouldn't be. Let me know if you hear anything. I'm going to the cafe for some lunch. Bye now." Jessie clicked off the call and swiveled her chair at the sound of a knock on her door.

"Come in," she called. She gaped at the figure in the doorway. "Well, to what do I owe this pleasure?"

Diane rushed in and shut the door. "I need to talk to you."

"Oh, do you have other clever insults to shower upon me?"

Diane looked over her shoulder as if she expected someone to grab her. "Listen, I don't have time to mess around. Lee is trying to convince everyone that Randy tampered with your car causing you to wreck."

"What? I already know Lee did it."

"Yes, but that's not the story he's telling. Do you want to hear me out?"

The look in Diane's eyes convinced Jessie to listen. "I think I've heard it, but continue."

Diane's voice wavered initially but grew stronger as she explained Lee's plot to get even with Jessie. Jessie listened to her silently until Diane reached the part about her visit to the fire station that morning.

"Hold on, Diane. So, you're saying you recorded Lee's story about Randy as you were telling it to Jordan and Jeremy then turned off the recording and told them the truth? That sounds like a crazy movie plot." She scrunched her face in confusion. "And how does a woman like you get involved with a narcissistic, misogynist like Lee?"

Diane looked directly at Jessie. "I was wondering the same about you."

Jessie paled. So, Diane knew about her fling with Lee. What else had he told her? "Me? I was a gullible file clerk who believed his sweet script." Jessie said with a bitter laugh. "But you? Why? How are you involved with Lee and his revenge against me?"

Diane's face crumpled as she slid into a chair close to Jessie. "It's a long story, but I got into trouble with a gambling debt, and Lee offered his lawyer services to help me out." She paused, her lips tight, "Let's just say it came with conditions."

"You? A gambler? Ha! I can't believe a saint like you would darken the doors of a casino. Or," she shot Diane a smug look, "agree to conditions."

"Do you want to hear the rest?"

"By all means."

"Jessie, Lee sent me to tell you a similar story about Randy, but I'm not doing that. I'm telling you the truth."

Jessie's eyes narrowed. "Why the sudden change of heart?"

"It isn't really sudden. I told Lee I wanted no part of this, but he owns me." She sniffled and wiped her nose. "I don't want to ruin anyone's life."

"That's rubbish! You've never liked me, Diane. And it's no secret you and Patrick hate Jeremy's vision for the church."

Diane stood and walked to the other side of the room. She stared out the window for several seconds, then turned to Jessie, her face etched with a look of terror. "I'm scared, Jessie. He's waiting for me to bring him the recording of our conversation. I don't know what he'll do when he finds out I didn't tell you his lies about Randy."

Unanticipated pity rose in Jessie for the woman whose trademark haughtiness had vanished, leaving her vulnerable as a child. "Okay, Diane. Tell me what's going on with you and Lee."

"Lee threatened to tell Patrick about my gambling debt if I didn't do everything he said."

"Is it worth it, though? Patrick might be upset, but I doubt he'd divorce you over a mistake like that."

"It amounted to thousands of dollars, but there's so much more. I've done terrible things, Jessie, things you wouldn't understand. But for the record, I had nothing to do with your accident. Lee bragged to me about it one night. That's how I know he's the one who caused it."

Jessie searched Diane's face. Diane knew of her past with Lee, but did she know of the incident buried deepest in her soul? "I might understand."

Regret played on Diane's features, and she began a tale that Jessie suspected she'd never revealed before. Dark deeds of stealing church money and a plot to destroy Jeremy's ministry poured from Diane's perfectly painted lips. And one final secret pierced Jessie like a knife.

Diane's voice trembled, and she leaned in. "I got pregnant, and Lee forced me to get an abortion, or else he'd expose my sins to the church. I'm a horrible person, Jessie. I never intended for any of this to happen."

"But— but are you sure the baby was Lee's?"

Diane nodded. "Patrick can't father children. So, he'd know it wasn't his."

Jessie could only stare at the broken woman crying out her anguish, trapped like a fly in Lee's web of threats and intimidation. A single tear leaked from Jessie's eye and trickled down her cheek. Diane's cool hand touched her arm.

"Jessie, I'm sorry about all of this."

Jessie shook herself. "This is so much. We need to decide what to do next. Is Lee waiting for you?"

"I'm supposed to see him in the morning, but I think he's losing confidence in me. He may try to get the recording today. Maybe we could make a fake one like I did when I told Jordan."

"We could. But I don't think in our emotional states we'd sound very plausible. Maybe we should call the police. Are you afraid to leave here?"

"Yes. I have no recording to give Lee. I guess I could tell him the app glitched."

"I doubt that would work. Jordan talked to a policeman about all this. He gave an officer Lee's jacket and the lug wrench."

Diane caught her breath. "That's what Lee's afraid of."

"Are you ready to tell the police what you know?"

"Only on the phone. I think I'll be safe here."

* * *

Lee drove around the visitors' parking lot until he spied Diane's car. He let out a long sigh of relief. So, she did come through. He found a place toward the back and waited. Acquiring that recording was worth the risk of being seen with her. Twenty minutes passed, and Lee drummed his fingers on the steering wheel. What was taking so long? Was Diane having trouble finding a moment of privacy to talk to Jessie? Or maybe she needed help convincing her to believe the story about Randy. He flung open the car door and climbed out. After all, he was an expert in the art of persuasion.

Lee asked for Jessie's room number at the front desk and found the way to her hall. Searching the top of each door, he spotted her number. The door was closed. The side of his neck tingled. Was Diane in there? A staff member turned the corner, and Lee continued to the end of the hallway. He could see Jessie's room, but he couldn't stand around waiting for it to open without drawing suspicion.

A rumbling in his stomach reminded Lee that he hadn't eaten all morning. He walked until he found the cafe. Not wanting to waste time standing in the lunch line, he settled for a sandwich from the vending machine. After he washed down the day-old turkey layered between dry bread, he decided to head back to Jessie's room.

The door was still closed, so he crept to it and pressed the side of his head against the wood. Mumbled sounds met his ear, but he couldn't tell who was speaking. It might be a staff member. Maybe he'd missed Diane somehow. Frustrated, he stepped away, but a familiar high-pitched voice caught his attention. His lips quivered as his hand twisted the doorknob.

* * *

Jordan and Jeremy returned from a wreck on the highway that involved multiple cars. Fortunately, none of the injuries were life-threatening. After ensuring the vehicles and equipment were ready for the next run, Jordan caught Jeremy's eye and motioned for him to follow. As they walked toward his office, Jordan spoke.

"I got a text from Trent as we were pulling in. Apparently, Diane went to Hope Rehab to see Jessie. Something went down because Jessie called the police saying Diane was ready to turn Lee in."

"Ah, I bet Lee demanded she tell Jessie the lie about Randy, too."

"That would be my guess, but she must have told her the truth instead."

"You think Diane's story to us was on the level, then?"

Jordan leaned against his office door frame. His forehead wrinkled in confusion. "Maybe, but if Diane's been involved with Lee, why would she suddenly change her tune and turn on him?"

"Who knows? But Jordan, you know Lee is a master

manipulator. Maybe he's blackmailing Diane for some reason, and she wants out. She told us she couldn't go through with his plan."

"Could be." He angled his head, "At any rate, Trent is going to Hope Rehab and take a statement from Diane. He'll hang around for a bit. Probably escort Diane home before picking up Lee."

Jeremy pounded his fist into his palm. "Dang! I wish we could be there."

"Me too, Preacher Boy, but Trent's a sharp guy. He'll take care of them." He gave Jeremy a playful tap and cracked a wry grin. "And watch your language, punk."

"Oh, shut up, or I'll unleash words that'd make a sailor blush."

"Whoa now! That'd be a red-letter day," Jordan laughed. "Let's go to lunch."

* * *

The door swung open, and Lee entered Jessie's room wearing a taunting smirk. "Hello, ladies. I hope I'm interrupting something," he said, closing the door behind him.

The color drained from Diane's face. "Oh!"

Jessie's hand reached into the open purse hanging from the arm of her chair. Her fingers rubbed the smoothness of the secret cylinder. "Why did you come here?"

Her nose wrinkled at the scent of chewed-up deli turkey as Lee leaned in close, his scornful smile inches from her face. "Why, Jessie, can't an old friend visit? I came to express my condolences for your accident. I just hate to see you incapacitated."

Jessie gripped the arm of her wheelchair, every

tendon in her hand aching to land a blow across his jaw. The fingers of her other hand tightened on the pepper spray. "Leave these premises before I call security and have you thrown out."

Lee righted himself. "Hmm. Never at a loss for words are you, dear?" He swung around. "Diane, I assume you've told Jessie about our findings." He clasped his hands together. "Poor old Randy, too stupid to realize I overheard his little secret."

Jessie glanced nervously toward the door. Where was Officer Trent? Needing to stall, she gestured to Lee. "Have a seat since you came to visit. Yes, Diane relayed your message about Randy, but it sounds a bit questionable. I'm still processing it."

Lee faced Diane. "Let's hear it, then. Give me your phone."

Diane cast a hopeless look at Jessie and handed the phone to Lee. "Here it is."

Lee grabbed the phone and tapped the playback button. Diane's conversation with Jordan and Jeremy played. "No, not that one!" His face shouted his frustration. "Where's the recording of your conversation with Jessie?"

Diane took the phone with trembling hands. She tapped it several times, her eyes glued on the screen. "I—I guess it didn't record for some reason. I know I turned it on."

"Give it here!" He messed with the phone briefly, then turned cold-blooded eyes to Diane. He grabbed her arm, giving it a hard squeeze. "You're lying! You'll regret that decision."

"Ow! You're hurting me."

Jessie's fingers searched for the canister's trigger. "Let go of her! She didn't need to record your lies. I'm aware of your crimes." She lifted the pepper spray from her purse, aiming it at Lee.

Lee flinched and pulled Diane close to his side. "What is that?"

With Diane so close to Lee, Jessie couldn't get off a shot without hitting her. "Let go of her, or I'll spray you both!"

Lee inched closer, dragging along his ashen-faced captive. He reached into his pocket, jerked out a switchblade, and popped it open. "Put it down, Jessie," he said in a menacing tone, "or I'll run this through that hand."

Jessie put her thumb under the triggering lever releasing the safety. "Back off! Don't underestimate me." She'd stop Lee or go down fighting.

Lee studied Jessie as if calculating his risk, but she held his gaze with unflinching eyes.

Uttering a guttural sound, Diane twisted her torso catching Lee off guard, then ground the heel of her shoe into his foot. He yowled and loosened his grip on Diane, who twisted from his grasp. Lee lunged toward Jessie. Her thumb flipped the trigger. The mist spurted out, striking Lee's face full stream. He crumpled to his knees, shrieking curses and rubbing his eyes. Fueled with terror-fed rage, Jessie sprayed until she drained the container.

Trent burst into the room with his gun drawn. Lee lay writhing on the floor. "That will do it, Jessie. We've got him."

Another officer handcuffed the wailing Lee and led him through the people gathered at the door. Trent holstered his weapon and addressed the crowd. "Everything's okay now. You can all go back to your duties."

Trent knelt and looked into Jessie's glazed eyes. "It's over now. You're one gusty lady." He touched her arm, still gripping the canister aimed at where Lee had fallen. Her pulse thudded against her temples, and her breaths came in rapid gulps. It was over. She released the canister, and it clattered against the floor.

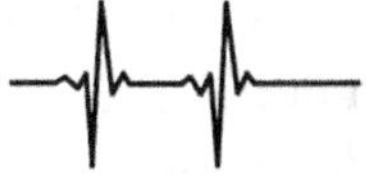

CHAPTER TWENTY-ONE

A week after Lee's arrest, Jordan arrived at Hope Rehabilitation Hospital to bring Jessie home. Vikki and Jeremy waited at Jessie's parents' house to celebrate her homecoming and help unload.

Jessie's eyes swept the lobby of Hope Rehabilitation Center, the place that had played such a vital role in her physical and emotional healing. Her heart swelled at the sight of medical professionals, therapists, and other staff gathered for her send-off. Each one had taught her, in different ways, to accept her new lifestyle. Becky knelt by her side, and Jessie clung to her for several seconds. "Never will I be able to express my gratitude for your compassion and encouragement. I'll miss you."

"You've been good for me, Jessie. My faith has grown from watching you."

Jessie wiped a tear from her eye. "I'll see you at the wedding, right?"

"I wouldn't miss it."

Jessie lifted her hand in a queen's wave and smiled as she rolled out the door into the light of the summer sun.

She raised questioning eyes to Jordan as he led her to a blue Trailblazer.

"Where's your truck?"

"I traded it in for this beauty. Do you like it?"

"Jordan, you loved your truck. You shouldn't have done that."

"Nah, I needed a change. You should be able to transfer easily and there's room to haul your wheelchair and other things we'll need."

"I know, but..." Jessie squeezed his hand, "Thank you. We'll get you another truck one day."

"Hmm. Maybe. If you like this, we can get it converted with hand controls, so you can drive it later on."

Jessie wiped the corner of her eye and hugged him. "That would be great."

Jordan helped Jessie transfer, then took off the wheels on her chair and loaded it in the back. He hopped in the driver's seat and grinned. "Let's blow this joint, Love."

* * *

Jordan sat with Jessie on his couch at the end of a busy moving day. After unloading necessary personal items at her parents' house, they packed some of Jessie's clothes from her apartment and brought them over.

Jessie's eyes seemed troubled, like they had a couple of times during the day, but she'd brushed off Jordan's concerns claiming exhaustion from the move and emotions the day had brought. Jordan wrapped his arms around her, "Just a couple of weeks, Love, and this will be your home."

Jessie smiled slightly and touched the tube that

drained into her leg bag. "After the procedure to remove my catheter tomorrow, Mom, Vikki, Mary, and I are going to finish shopping for the wedding. We're picking up my dress from the seamstress who altered it for the wheelchair."

"That sounds like a fun girls' day." Jordan's eyes fell on the bag that collected Jessie's urine. "You'll feel better without that, I'm sure. Are you anxious about using an intermittent catheter yourself?"

"Not really, the nurses had me practice. It's one of the many things I've had to learn."

"Well, then, I guess you'll have a lot to teach me."

Jessie's lips turned up in a flirty grin. "Oh, I thought you'd done your research."

Jordan widened his eyes in a look of shocked innocence. "Why, Jessie, I'm surprised at you. I meant teach me about your procedures."

Jessie tilted her head. "What else would I teach you? I've no clue about what you're implying."

"Sure, you don't." He held her, captivated by the scent of her perfume. "I love you, Jessie."

"And I love you."

Jordan willed his arms to let her go. "We probably need to be getting you home, so you can get plenty of rest for tomorrow."

"It should be a simple procedure, but I will need to get up early."

Jordan grinned. "Yeah, and you'll want to be rested for your big shopping day."

Jessie straightened her frame and faced him. Her brown eyes, flecked with amber, held the same troubled expression he'd noticed earlier. "Are you ok, Love? Do we need to talk about something?"

"I'm fine, just fatigued. It's been an emotional day."

Jordan searched her face. She looked tired, yes, but there was something else, something she was holding back. He brought her hand to his lips. "Jessie, I love you. Please tell me what's bothering you."

Jessie looked past him. "I'm fine. We can talk later. You need to get up early too."

Jordan sighed. He hated waiting, but Jessie wasn't ready to share her thoughts. He tried to convince himself that it was only weariness he saw, but there was something more behind her eyes, something she wasn't telling him. Was she in doubt about their wedding plans again? Hopefully, they were beyond that, and she realized his level of commitment, knowing he would never feel she wasn't enough. He kissed her gently, fighting the urge to draw her closer, and pulled her wheelchair to the couch. "Let's get you to your mom and dad's," he said, avoiding the word home. This house would be her home.

* * *

Jessie woke up early the following day, excited but anxious at the prospect of getting rid of the catheter and urine bag she'd dealt with for nearly two months. She was awake and ready on time with the assistance of her mother. She only had to freshen up before they left.

It promised to be a great day. After the procedure, she would pick up her wedding dress and enjoy a shopping trip. She'd scaled her previous wedding list down to a size the chapel at Hope Rehabilitation could accommodate and planned a reception at New Life Community Church for a larger crowd. So, a fun, relaxing day for everyone to try on their dresses and make final preparations lay ahead of her.

It should be fun, except for the dark cloud hanging over it— the truth she must share with Jordan. She shoved that thought away when she heard Mary and Vikki's voices. This day was for celebration. She smiled and rolled into the living room, where her mother and friends were chatting.

Vikki smiled as Jessie came into the room. "Are you ready to go? Mary brought our grandparent's van with a ramp, so you can stay in your chair and won't have to worry about transferring each stop."

"Thank you, Mary. Not having to transfer will be helpful."

Jessie's procedure went well, and afterward, the ladies enjoyed lunch at Jessie's favorite Mexican restaurant. Sitting in the dining room decorated with a brightly colored mural painted on the walls and listening to the lively chatter at the table struck Jessie with awe. The surroundings felt normal yet remarkable, ordinary but precious. She dipped a chip in salsa and crunched it, savoring its saltiness mixed with spicy salsa. Her eyes closed, cherishing the sense of freedom that threatened to overwhelm her.

Marianne touched her daughter's hand. "What's wrong, dear? Is something hurting you?"

Jessie shook her head. "No, Mom, just soaking in the atmosphere. It's fabulous."

When they finished shopping, Marianne invited everyone for dessert. Vikki sat with Jessie on the patio while Marianne showed Mary her flower garden.

"How are you feeling being on your feet all day?" Jessie asked, noticing Vikki touch her side as she sat down.

"Not bad, really. Still a little tender, but much better than a week ago."

"I'm glad to hear that." Jessie twisted the engagement ring on her finger. "Vikki, I made an appointment to talk with Brandon about what I shared with you the other day. Will you drive me to the church?"

"Well yes, of course, but why? I mean, haven't you told Jordan?"

"No, the timing never seemed right. I thought Brandon could offer his counsel, but if you don't think I should…"

"I didn't mean it that way. If you want to talk to Brandon, that's fine. And I'll go with you if you want me to. It's just I thought you'd already prayed for — "

"I have prayed, and I know I don't need to confess to Brandon. I guess I just need his affirmation that I'm forgiven."

"You're forgiven, Jessie. But I'll go with you. We can load your wheelchair in the back of my car."

Jessie squeezed Vikki's hand. "You're a true friend. Thank you."

* * *

Jordan needed to check in with Jeremy about a supply inventory sheet after the day's training session. He found him sitting at a table in the lounge, reading his Bible and writing notes on his laptop. "Prepping for Sunday?"

Jeremy nodded. "It's my week to bring the message."

"Just wondered if you'd signed off on the inventory sheet."

"Yep. It's been checked and filed."

"Thanks. Have you heard anymore about what's going on with Lee?"

"No, but I did have a talk with Diane."

Jordan sank into the chair next to Jeremy. "That sounds dangerous."

Jeremy chuckled. "Not just me, of course. Brandon met with Diane, Patrick, and myself."

"Does Patrick know about Diane's gambling debt and her shenanigans with Lee?"

"Yes, she'd already told him. Patrick agreed to counseling in an attempt to save their marriage. Brandon called the meeting to clear the air about everything that's gone on."

Jordan frowned. "It would be hard to forgive that kind of betrayal."

"I know, but Diane regrets everything and seems truly repentant. I think one deceitful action led to another until it spiraled out of control. She was in so deep that she couldn't find a way out."

"Yeah, I was shocked when Jessie filled us in on Diane's involvement with Lee. The level of control Lee wielded over her is astounding."

"Narcissistic people like him have a way of doing that. Diane did come clean in the end though and helped bring Lee to justice."

Jordan took a deep breath, picturing Jessie's face when the doctor told her she would never walk again. "Lee's harmed enough people. I hope he is locked up for a long time."

"Me too." Jeremy looked at Jordan as if he wanted to say more.

"What is it, Preacher Boy?"

"We all had a good discussion during the meeting. Diane asked for my forgiveness and plans to make amends to everyone she's wronged. I apologized, too."

Jordan eyed him with surprise. "Whatever for?"

"My attitude and childish name-calling at the benefit."

"Get real, Jeremy. Don't you think she had it coming?"

Jeremy smiled. "Yes, but in Brandon's eyes name calling is 'unbecoming' for a preacher, or any Christian for that matter. He's right, you know, and I figured an apology from me wouldn't hurt."

Jordan lifted his eyes. "Oh, brother. Well, if you ever find yourself in a situation like that again, do me a favor and come up with a stronger word. I mean, if you have to apologize for swearing, it should be a tad more vulgar than punk."

Jeremy laughed. "I'll give it my best shot."

Jordan's phone chimed. "I've got a text from Jessie. Hmm. Apparently, we're meeting with Brandon after I get off work."

"Maybe something about the wedding."

"No doubt. Brandon probably wants to give me last minute instructions so I won't be an 'unbecoming husband'," he said with a cocky grin.

* * *

Jordan rang the bell and waited for the release click. He walked toward the light shining from Brandon's office. Surprised to see Vikki with the other two, he stopped in the doorway and lifted his eyebrows at Jessie. "I thought this was about our upcoming wedding, but I guess I'm wrong." He grinned. "Unless there's something I don't know about." Brandon's somber face caught his eye, "Mmm, sorry."

"Come in Jordan," Brandon said with a thin smile

and pointed to the seat next to Jessie, "We'd like you to join our little chat."

Jordan sat in the chair. The atmosphere seemed overly tense for the informality Brandon assigned it. "Is something wrong?" Jessie avoided his gaze, but the look in Vikki's eyes gave him the answer.

Brandon cleared his throat. "Jordan, out of respect for you and the importance of honesty in your relationship, Jessie feels the need to tell you something. Vikki and I are here to support her."

Jessie glanced his way with an expression that made Jordan's heart skip a beat. Was she sick? Having second thoughts about their wedding? "What is it?"

Brandon stood, and Vikki followed his lead. He looked directly at Jordan. "Please understand that Jessie is going to share something that will cost her deeply, but her motivation comes from love." He looked at Vikki, "We'll wait in the conference room."

Alone in the room, Jessie looked at him with hollow eyes. "I'm sorry I asked you to come here, but I needed a neutral place, and Brandon suggested his office since Vikki and I were already here."

Jordan's brow twisted in confusion. "Is Vikki part of whatever this is?"

"No, she drove me here and stayed while I met with Brandon." Jessie bit her bottom lip. "I'm not sure how to tell you this."

Jordan couldn't ignore the dread rising in him. "Are you breaking up with me?"

A tear leaked from the corner of Jessie's eye. "No, but you may want to after what I tell you."

"That won't happen."

Jessie closed her eyes for a moment as if gathering

courage. When she finally spoke, Jordan had to lean in to hear her .

"After my— encounter with Lee," she paused momentarily, squeezing her fingers, then her words rushed out. "I got pregnant, and Lee insisted on termination."

Jordan caught his breath as his brain processed her words. Abortion. The secret she couldn't muster the courage to share last night. His eyes searched her face for some sign he'd misunderstood.

Jessie swiped at her tears, and her eyes collided with his. "You can't handle that can you?" she said, defiance in her tone. "You think I'm a murderer. After all, your mom runs the crisis pregnancy center, and you drove around with a pro-life bumper sticker on your truck."

"No, I…" Jordan massaged his temples. As much as Jessie's confession shocked him, her accusing tone is what cut into the core of his being. His pro-life stance was no secret, but at this moment, the anguished look on the face of the woman he loved made him blink away tears.

"Give me a minute," he murmured, sliding his chair directly in front of her wheelchair. Taking her hands, he worked his fingers between hers. "I don't have the words I need." Closing his eyes, he lifted a silent prayer for understanding and wisdom. He felt impressed with the need to hear her story. "Talk to me, Love. Tell me about it."

Jessie wiped fresh tears with the tissue Jordan offered. "I found out very early that I was pregnant. I was stupid to let myself be put in that situation and naive enough to think Lee cared for me."

"What did he say when you told him you were pregnant?"

"He was livid. Called me an irresponsible slut."

Anger stiffened Jordan's jaw. "Like he had nothing to do with it."

"He told me I would be an embarrassment to my father. The church elders would declare him unfit for ministry since he was unable to raise a virtuous daughter." She swallowed, her eyes brimming, "I couldn't face my family, Jordan. I couldn't drag my father and mother through the mud. My father didn't fail. I did."

"And I bet Lee escorted you to the clinic, right?" Jordan said through pursed lips.

"Oh, yes. That morning he brought me flowers and told me he had feelings for me, but we were star crossed. That he regretted this had to be done. Assured me it was the only option to save my family from embarrassment. Said someday we'd be together." Jessie's face contorted.

"But you know what? He abandoned me." She drew in two quick breaths. "When the deed was done, he left me there, utterly alone. I had to call a taxi to get home."

Anger simmered in the depths of Jordan's soul. "What kind of human does something like that? I've never hated anyone until now."

"Hating him won't help, Jordan. Believe me."

"But he lied to you, manipulated you, nearly destroyed you. More than once."

"That's true, Jordan, but in the end, it was my decision. I made a regrettable choice. But Brandon assured me of God's grace. I just don't know if you can forgive me."

Jordan sighed. Would she never fully trust his love? He wheeled her over to the couch. "I need to hold you," he said. "Please." He helped her transfer and pulled her onto his lap. His fingers traced her forehead. "Jessie, you've made your peace with God. What right do I have to pass judgment? God's grace is all anyone needs." He twisted a stray curl around his finger. "I respect your decision to tell me, and it only makes me love you more. What saddens me is that you believed I would leave you." He kissed her forehead. "You're stuck with me, Love." His finger touched her cheek, erasing a stray tear. "I'm curious, though, why you decided to tell me now. Has it been weighing on your mind?"

"Not until recently. Actually, I had repressed the whole ordeal so much that I rarely thought of it. It was there, though, and I planned to tell you someday." She met Jordan's eyes.

"Lee did the same thing to Diane, Jordan."

"No way. You mean got her pregnant and— "

"Yes, and bullied her into an abortion. She's kept the same secret, and it's damaged her on so many levels."

Jordan's jaw dropped. "I won't say a word. It's her story. And yours is yours. No one else needs to know."

"Absolutely. Besides you, only Vikki and Brandon know. I've given Vikki permission to tell Jeremy. Brandon suggested I might share my experience as a ministry someday. I'm not ready for that." She sniffed. "But I may be someday."

Jessie wrapped her arms around Jordan's neck, and he brought her closer. He kissed her softly on the cheek. "Let's get married now, Love. Brandon's right down the hall."

Jessie giggled. "Are you serious?"

"Kinda. But no, I want to see you walk, uh, I mean roll down the aisle."

"Well, I guess I could lie on the floor. It does slant. And if my dad nudges me, I might roll."

Jordan's heart fluttered at the sound of her laughter.

She was still the feisty girl he'd fallen in love with under the moonlit night of their first date. "I love you, Jessie," he said, brushing his lips against hers.

A tentative knock sounded on the door, and it cracked open. "Is everything ok?"

"Yeah, come in," Jordan said and kissed her again.

Brandon raised one eyebrow and exchanged glances with Vikki, "Are we breaking in on something?"

"No. Not yet anyway," Jordan said with a roguish grin.

Jessie scooted off Jordan's lap and punched his leg.

Brandon stared at him, then his mouth lifted in a boyish grin. "Well, it looks as if you've worked everything out."

CHAPTER TWENTY-TWO

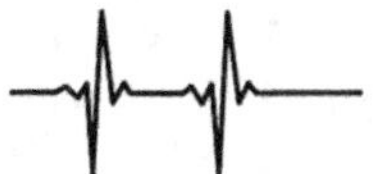

Jessie awoke to the sound of a running vacuum and a touch of cool air on her face. She smiled to herself. Her mother was adding the final touches to her already immaculate house for any guests who might stop by. She stretched her arms and thought of the fateful morning a few months ago that changed her life forever. But memories were for another time. Today she would marry Jordan, the man who'd stood by her through all her frustration and doubts as she sought purpose in her new life.

Marianne appeared in her doorway. "Good morning, dear. I opened your window earlier. There's a nice breeze this morning."

"Yes, it feels wonderful, thank you."

"Well, this is your big day," Marianne said, patting Jessie's arm. "Are you ready for it to begin?"

"Absolutely."

Jessie transferred to her chair and went into the bathroom adjoining her parents' bedroom, the only one with a wide enough door for her wheelchair. Marianne gathered towels and helped Jessie reach the items she needed. "I'm so grateful that your church members helped make Jordan's house accessible for you."

"Yes, they are amazing. And so are you and Dad. Thanks again for allowing me the use of your room."

Marianne hesitated in the doorway. "Jessie, I want you to know how happy I am for you. Your father and I think the world of Jordan." She wiped a finger under her eyes. "I never doubted his love for you. I was afraid for you."

Jessie reached for her mother's hand. "It's ok, Mom. I know you always want the best for me. It's been an overwhelming time for everyone."

Marriane squeezed Jessie's shoulders and smiled. "You and Jordan will be fine. He is a good man."

"He is that."

The doorbell rang. "I bet that's Vikki."

"Yes, I told her to come early, so we could relax and take our time preparing for the day."

"Good, I baked a breakfast casserole for us when you're ready."

"Thanks, Mom. I love you."

After eating Marianne's delicious breakfast and reviewing the day's plans, the three ladies drove to Hope Rehab, where Jessie would finish her hair and makeup in a visitor's lounge next to the chapel.

* * *

Jeremy and Robbie sat at the local cafe in a booth across from Jordan. Jeremy stabbed a chunk of pancake. "Well, this is it, Jordan. How are you holding up? In a few hours, you'll be a married man."

Jordan held up his hands. "I surrender. Drag me to the altar."

Jeremy laughed. "Yeah, right. She's forcing your hand. You're hopeless, ya know."

"Help me out here, Preacher Boy," Jordan said with a sideways glance at Robbie, "I'm trying to hold on to a shred of dignity."

"Nooo, it's too late for that," Robbie teased. "You're lovesick, dude. I hear Jessie's the one who needed convincing." He raised his glass in a toast. "Seriously though, I wish you all the happiness in the world."

"Thanks, Robbie." Jordan said, lifting his coffee mug. "So, tell us, when are you going to put a ring on Mary's finger?"

Robbie brushed a lock of blond hair from his shoulder. "Soon. I've actually picked one out."

Jordan gave the table a gentle slap with his fist. "What's the hold up, rock star?"

"Nothing really, I'll give it to her after your wedding. I want to see how this goes for you first."

"Sure thing. I'll give you an update. Probably not tonight, though. I might have plans. Besides, I'm not the kiss-and-tell type." Jordan held his hand to the corner of his mouth and whispered, "But maybe tomorrow."

Robbie high-fived him. "I'll give you a call."

Jordan caught Jeremy's *I can't believe you said that* look. "Watch out, Robbie, or we'll be the subject of one of Preacher Boy's sermons."

"Well, with you around, I'll never lack material," Jeremy said as he grabbed the bill. "Come on, Robbie, let's tie Romeo up and drag him to the chapel."

* * *

Jessie, her bridesmaids, and her flower girl, Heather, posed for pictures. Vikki and Mary wore royal blue tea-length dresses with lace trim on the bodice and capped sleeves. Heather's dress was the same shade of blue with a yellow ribbon around the waistband. Their dresses complimented Jessie's lacy tea-length gown with a blue silk sash wrapped around her waist. The bridesmaids carried a yellow and white rose tied with a blue ribbon. Jessie's bouquet consisted of baby's breath and yellow roses gathered with a blue ribbon.

Jessie breathed in the fragrance of flowers arranged in silver vases on each end of the stage. Yellow roses bound with white ribbons graced the end of the pews. It was here, the moment she'd longed for, feared, and sometimes barely believed could happen. God had mended all the shattered pieces of her heart and led her to this moment. In less than an hour, she would be Jordan's wife.

* * *

Jordan, dressed in a black suit with a light blue vest and tie, walked to the front of the chapel with Jeremy and Robbie. Music played, and Heather tossed flowers with abandonment, her golden curls bouncing as she skipped down the aisle. Mary began her walk with Robbie meeting her halfway and escorting her to the front of the chapel. Then Jeremy stepped out and walked toward the back to meet Vikki.

Frank touched Jessie's shoulder. "Are you ready, honey?"

Jessie smiled up at him, "Yes."

Frank bent over and hugged his daughter. "I love

you, Jessie and pray for God's blessing on you and Jordan."

"Thanks, Dad." Jessie squeezed his strong hand and dabbed her eyes. "You've modeled a great marriage for me. I love you."

Jessie and her father started down the aisle. She found Jordan's eyes and held them for a long moment. He grinned and gave her a thumbs-up. A giggle slipped past her lips. As she approached, Jordan sat down in a chair to await her, and the attendants also took a seat. Jessie's heart swelled at the sweet gesture. It was so like Jordan, spirited and irreverent, yet sensitive, with a heart of gold. What good thing had she done to deserve him?

Jessie's dad positioned her in front of Jordan's chair. Jordan took her hands, his dark eyes glowing. "You're breathtaking, Love."

Brandon stepped to the podium. "Friends and family of Jordan Raycom and Jessie Marcus, welcome. We are gathered here today to witness the marriage of this man and this woman whose love has been tested, yet endured, and found a way to thrive through adversity."

He read from 1st Corinthians chapter 13, verses 4-8. "Love is patient, love is kind. It does not envy, it does not boast, it is not proud. It does not dishonor others, it is not self-seeking, it is not easily angered, it keeps no record of wrong. Love does not delight in evil but rejoices in truth. It always protects, always trusts, always hopes, always preserves. Love never fails"

Brandon addressed the wedding party. "Jordan, wishes to speak some words to his bride."

Jessie's cheeks warmed at this turn of events. She hadn't planned any personal vows.

Jordan squeezed her hands as if reassuring her and gazed into her eyes. "Jessie, no words could adequately describe how you've rocked my world from the moment my eyes caught a glimpse of your lovely face." He caught Jermey's eye with a subtle wink. "And I'm forever grateful that after asking Jeremy if he knew the hot chick across the church lobby, he actually introduced me to you. Though, for some reason, he felt it necessary to warn me that you were his sister." He paused as giggles rose from the crowd. "Saying I waited all my life for you may sound cliche, but it's true. God gave me the love I thought I'd never know." His voice broke, and he paused. "You complete me. You're my soulmate and I love you."

Jessie blinked rapidly, but an unchecked tear trickled from the corner of her eye. This man never ceased to amaze her. "Thank you," she whispered.

Jeremy stepped up to lead them through their vows. Jessie soaked in the love radiating from Jordan's eyes, and the soft caress of his fingers steadied her as they repeated Jeremy's words of commitment. He finished with, "I now pronounce you man and wife. Jordan, you may kiss your bride."

Jordan lifted his hand in a sassy salute. "Yes, sir, Preacher." Laughter bubbled up from the audience. He met Jessie's lips with a tender kiss. She grinned at him. He truly was irrepressible. "You always make me laugh," she whispered.

"How romantic," Jordan said with a crooked grin.

Brandon offered a prayer of blessing on their union and ended the ceremony. Jessie waved to the crowd as Jordan walked beside her chair. They made their way down the aisle to the courtyard, where a tent had been set up for a small reception before the celebration at the church that evening.

Jordan and Jessie mingled with the crowd greeting their guests. Jessie spotted Elizabeth and John outside the tent and maneuvered her chair toward them. "I'm so pleased you came."

Elizabeth held out her hand. "We've been looking forward to it. You look lovely and the ceremony was beautiful."

John smiled at her. "Elizabeth's right. You and Jordan exuded joy walking down the aisle."

"Thank you, we're very happy." Jessie looked at Elizabeth. "Your words the night of the benefit touched me, both the ones from the stage and from our conversation in the church. You taught me so much in the few minutes we shared. It changed my perspective and gave me hope."

"It was my pleasure. Any opportunity God gives me to share my story to help someone on their journey is a blessing to me."

Jordan strolled up to the group. "Thanks for coming. It's good to see you again."

John shook his hand. "Congratulations. You've got yourself a great wife."

"You bet. I married up, that's for sure. Will we see you at the party over at the church in a bit?"

"We'll be there."

* * *

Jessie, Jordan, and the wedding party headed to Jordan's house to change clothes before the evening festivities on the church lawn. The girls helped Jessie transfer onto the bed and change into dark blue jeans and a glittery silver off-the-shoulder top.

"It seems like you're doing well with everything

you've had to learn Jessie," Mary said. "I never realized how many adjustments you'd have to make."

"That's understandable. I had no idea either until it happened to me. It's a whole new set of life skills to master. But the most difficult thing to learn was that I'm still me, and it's ok."

"Yes, and you're incredible. So strong."

"It's not my strength, Mary. God placed people on my path that led me out of despair and into hope."

Jordan knocked on the half-opened door and peeked around the corner. "Are you ladies ready?"

"Five minutes."

They loaded into Jordan's new Trailblazer a few minutes later and headed to the church. Friends and family were adding the final touches to the food tables and decorations under the white canopy. The aroma of sizzling hamburgers floated in the air. Robbie and his band were setting up nearby.

Jessie smiled up at Jordan. "The weather's marvelous, not too hot and a nice breeze. A beautiful late summer evening."

"Yes, Love. It's a perfect day."

CHAPTER TWENTY-THREE

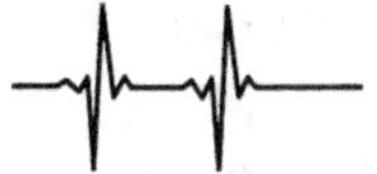

Jessie and Jordan wandered the grounds chatting with their guests. Jessie spotted Aiden hanging out with a few teens from church and waved.

"It's Jessie!" one of the girls shouted as the group ran up to them. "I'm so glad to see you. You look beautiful! I love your sparkly blouse."

"Thank you. It's good to see all of you, too. I've missed everyone."

The girls chatted with Jessie while the boys joked around with Jordan. Aiden and a girl with long wavy hair walked up to Jessie as the teens drifted away. A gift bag dangled from Aiden's hand.

"Hi, Aiden. You look nice. I like the haircut."

"Yeah, I got a few inches lopped off. My dad said I was scruffy looking."

"Well, it's a great look," Jessie said, exchanging a glance with the girl beside him. "Who's your friend?"

"Oh, um, yeah. This is Krista."

Jessie smiled and extended her hand. "My pleasure. I'm Jessie and this is uh… Jordan."

"Her husband," Jordan said, winking at Krista, "It's a fairly new concept for her."

Krista giggled. "It's nice to meet both of you."

Aiden held out the bag to Jessie. "Here, this is for you."

"Thank you, Aiden. Shall I open it now?"

"Sure, I mean, if you want to."

"Of course." Jessie peered in the bag. "Oh, Aiden." Tears came to her eyes as she pulled out a fluffy brown bear adorned with a blue bow around its neck. A tag attached to the bow read "I'm beary glad you're better," written in black ink. She pressed it against her cheek. "I love it."

Aiden shifted his gaze for a second, then looked at Jessie. "I wanted to give you this one in person."

Jessie's heart melted as she studied the young man who'd accepted undeserved guilt and put himself in danger to help bring the true culprit to justice. She reached out for his hand. "Thank you. It means a lot to me."

Aiden nodded and looked toward a group of young people hanging out near the stage. "Well, I uh, guess we'll see you later."

"Go have some fun, and… thank you again."

Jordan grasped Aiden's hand. "You're a good man, Aiden."

Aiden's eyes lit up, and he stood a bit straighter. "Thank you, Jordan." He reached for Krista's hand. "See you later."

"Well, Love," Jordan said as Aiden walked away, "I think we're wanted on the dance floor. Jeremy's hailing us."

Jessie hesitated. "We never practiced dancing. I might run over your feet."

"I'll watch out for you. We'll figure it out," Jordan said with a grin. "Come on."

People gathered around as Jordan and Jessie took their place in the middle of the dance floor, positioned on the lawn outside the tent. The band played a lively song, and Robbie's clear tenor rang out. Jessie looked up and met Jordan's eyes, soaking in his confidence. "Here we go," she whispered.

Jordan twirled her chair as he circled it. Jessie blew him a kiss and moved her upper body in time with Jordan's as they faced the crowd. To her delight, Jordan grabbed another wheelchair from the corner and plopped in it. He rolled close to Jessie and twisted until his chair spun around. Jessie swiveled her chair, and they performed a hilariously awkward dance for a cheering audience.

Worn out from more movement than she'd had in months, Jessie welcomed the following number, a slow love song. Jordan shed his chair and pushed Jessie's as they swayed to the beat. Other guests joined in, and the dance continued.

When the song ended, Jordan bent to Jessie's level. "Need a break?"

"Yes, I'm beat. I could use a bottle of water."

"I know, Love. I leave you breathless," Jordan said, dancing to the cooler.

* * *

Jessie and Jordan meandered through the crowd visiting with friends and family. After a couple of hours, Jordan went to look for Jeremy, who had offered to chauffeur them home. He spotted him a little way from the crowd embracing Vikki in a slow dance. Jeremy dipped his head and kissed his wife.

"Hey now, Preacher Boy. Better cool it. Brandon might think that's 'unbecoming' behavior for a preacher." He turned his head to both sides. "I think he has spies everywhere."

Jeremy dropped his hands. "Obviously." He peered over Jordan's shoulder. "Jessie ditch you already?"

"Funny, Preacher. Actually, I think we're about ready for you to take us to our honeymoon cottage. That is if you can tear yourself away."

"I'll manage. I bet Jessie's tired by now."

"Yeah, and we wouldn't want her to be too tired," Jordan said with a mischievous lift of his eyes. "I'll find Jessie and text you when we're headed to her vehicle." He nudged Jeremy closer to Vikki. "Carry on. You might step behind that tree, though. It's more private."

"Go away."

Jordan snickered. "Sure thing, Preacher Boy," he said with a wink.

Jordan walked through the crowd until he found Jessie sitting at one of the tables, talking with his parents. After a few minutes of conversation, Jordan stroked Jessie's arm.

"Are you about ready to go, Love?"

"Whenever you are. I've had a great time, but I haven't been at a social event for quite a while. My stamina's still lacking a little."

They said their goodbyes and headed to the Trailblazer. "How about I push you, Jessie? I'm sure you're tired."

"That would be fabulous."

They arrived at the meeting place before Jeremy and Vikki. Jessie looked up at Jordan. "I hope you aren't having second thoughts about putting off our wedding trip for a few months."

Jordan stooped so that he was level with her eyes and placed his hands on her shoulders, forever grateful that God had seen fit to allow her in his life. "All I want is to be with you, Jessie. It doesn't matter where." He touched her cheek. "I promise we'll go on a real honeymoon when you're stronger."

Jessie reached for his hand. "I'm perfectly happy to call your home our honeymoon cottage. Being with you is what matters."

Kneeling under the moonlit sky, Jordan couldn't tear his eyes away from his bride. "I remember the night of our first date, sharing a kiss in Vikki's driveway. It was a night like this one. You were beautiful with the breeze moving through your hair, like you are right now. I felt a connection from the beginning. And by some miracle, you fell in love with me."

"God sent you to me, Jordan. I believe that. He has a knack of bringing people I need into my life." Her eyes glistened. "But I'm a slow learner it seems."

"Nah, God's with us on our journey. We all need guidance."

Jeremy and Vikki walked up. "Hi. Ready to go?"

"Yep, whisk us away to our destination, Preacher."

CHAPTER TWENTY-FOUR

Jeremy pulled the Trailblazer up to Jordan's house, and Vikki followed in her car. A garland with the words Welcome Newlyweds hung across the porch. Blue and gold lights twinkled on the front railing and porch pillars.

"Welcome to your honeymoon cottage." Jeremy hopped out and sprinted to open the car door. "Your door keys, sir."

Jordan handed over his keys and helped Jessie transfer. He pointed to the porch. "Nice touch, Preacher."

"Thank Vikki and Mary. It was all their doing." Jeremy said, unlocking the front door. He bowed. "You may enter."

Jessie's eyes shone as she gazed at Jeremy and Vikki. "It's all amazing! Won't you come in?"

Jordan's eyes rounded like saucers, but he raised his hands with palms up. "Why not? It's early. We have time to kill."

Jeremy shot him a stifled grin. "No thanks. Another time."

Jordan and Jessie waved goodbye and entered their honeymoon destination. A sweet fragrance drew them to the kitchen, where yellow and white roses decorated the table.

"Look over here, Jordan."

A spread of refreshments with mugs and several coffee choices lay on one end of the counter. A box of pastries and flowered paper plates sat next to it. Jordan wrapped his arm around her shoulder. "For our breakfast, Love."

"That's so nice." Jessie squeezed his hand. "I think I'll freshen up a bit."

She wheeled down the hallway toward the bedroom, and Jordan followed, wondering what other surprises were waiting for them. He wasn't disappointed. Replacing the old, blue-striped bedspread he'd had since he moved in was a teal and ivory comforter. On the pillow shams lay round pieces of chocolate with rose petals scattered among them.

Jordan raised his eyebrows, "nice."

"Yes, the comforter is beautiful. And look," Jessie said, holding up a lacy nightgown. "My nighttime attire."

"Yeah, I might have to help you with that."

"Actually, putting clothes on is sometimes easier for me than getting them off."

"I'm versatile."

"I'm going to go to the restroom and wash up a bit. Then perhaps you'll help me transfer onto the bed."

"It's a deal," Jordan said, captivated by the rare blush rising on her cheeks.

Jordan removed the roses and chocolates from the pillows and folded the comforter to the end of the bed.

Jessie finished in the bathroom and wheeled herself to the bedside. Jordan guided the transfer board under her hips. He held the chair steady as she slid onto the bed, remembering his first awkward attempt to help her transfer at the rehab center.

Jessie settled herself and pointed to the chair. "If you hand the gown to me and help me get these jeans off, I'll be able to put it on."

Amused at her spunkiness, Jordan dangled the nightgown just out of her reach. "What's it worth to you?"

"Not a whole lot. I can sleep in my jeans, and I believe there's a spare bedroom for you."

Jordan snickered and handed her the gown. He tugged the jeans off her legs and helped her sit up. "That was fun," he said and kissed her nose. "Now what?"

"I can manage the rest." Jessie gave him a shy smile. "Will you wait in the living room? I want to get ready alone, and then I'll call for you."

Jordan arched his eyebrows. "Call for me? Hmm, I don't know," he said and played with the sleeve of her shirt. "It might be more interesting if I stay."

Jessie caught his hand. "Go away or this may be as interesting as it gets."

He kissed her cheek and stood up. "You're the second person to tell me to go away today." He grabbed a piece of chocolate. "I guess I'll change in the other room. Don't forget to call me."

Jordan leaned back on the recliner in the living room after changing into boxer shorts and a t-shirt. He closed his eyes. Married. The husband of a lovely lady that somehow fell in love with a guy like him. Beautiful, intelligent, and feisty, she'd stolen his heart from their first kiss.

He'd kept his promise to God, and it hadn't been difficult until he met Jessie. Her kisses electrified him, but they'd honored their commitment to wait. The accident had delayed their wedding, even threatened it. But that was all in the past. Jessie was in his bedroom, slipping into a silky pink nightgown.

"I'm ready."

"That doesn't sound much like a call."

"Jordan, my love, come to me."

Jordan waltzed into the room. "Here I am, darling. Prince Charming awaits your every desire."

Jessie gave him a faint smile and brushed unruly waves from her rosy cheeks. Her gown hung at a crooked angle over her left shoulder and bunched at the waist. She appeared slightly out of breath. "Hi."

Jordan bit his lips together, but his eyes held amusement. "Did you have a little trouble donning your gown, princess?" He climbed on the bed. "Let me help you."

He straightened the gown and drew her into a slow kiss. "Jessie, I love you."

Jessie framed his face with her hands. "I love you, too." She reached for something lying beside her. "Here, Jordan. These are yours, I believe."

Jordan stared at the familiar-looking keys in his hands. "What are these for?"

Jessie beamed. "Your truck. I purchased it from the dealer where you traded it in for the Trailblazer."

"But— "

"I used the insurance money I got for my Mustang."

The love, anticipation and beauty of the day mingled in Jordan's soul. He touched his mouth and his voice trembled. "Jessie, you shouldn't have. I— "

"I wanted to, Jordan. It's my wedding gift to you."

"But I have nothing for you."

"You've given me so much, Jordan."

"Thank you, Love." He wrapped her in his arms, pulled her down beside him, and his lips touched hers. She lay her head on his shoulder, and he drew in his breath, intoxicated by the scent of her hair and the warmth of her skin through the silky nightgown. He kissed her again and caressed her arms. His hand touched her leg before he remembered she couldn't feel it. His fingers lingered there, and he knew the truth at that moment. Even if things never went further, holding her this way would be enough. She would always be enough.

Jessie's feather-soft fingertips traced his jaw, and her eyes melted into his. "Are you okay, Jordan?"

"I'm — I'm not sure how— with your— "

Jessie traced his lips with her finger, her eyes full of mischief. "Figure it out, babe."

Jordan's lips turned up in a wide smile, "Okay, Love." He twisted a curl around his finger, then gathered his bride in his arms and loved her.

ACKNOWLEDGMENTS

Thank you to~
    Liz, my beta reader, friend and so much more
    Dave, my husband and encourager, I love you
    All the staff at Zamiz Press for believing in me
    "Love Lifted Me" © 1912, James Rowe

ABOUT THE AUTHOR

Broken Warriors is Cynthia Terrell's second novel set in the town of Claymon. Before becoming an author, Cynthia taught elementary students and continues to work with children. She and her husband Dave have two grown children and one granddaughter. *Broken Chains* was Cynthia's first book and was a story she had in her heart for several years.

You can connect with Cynthia and find out about her upcoming books at her website:

author-cynthia-jo-terrell.yolasite.com